Rich boy,
Poor boy

Rich boy,
Poor boy

by Theodora DuBois

(McCormick)

CANCELLED

ARIEL BOOKS

FARRAR, STRAUS AND CUDAHY

NEW YORK

To Sara Clarenbach

Rich boy,
Poor boy

1

The air was filled with the good September smell of bonfires and goldenrod, of sun-warmed pine trees and of late
summer roses from a flower border along the hedge. It
was pleasant on the Barrows' terrace. There were new
metal and plastic chairs, and glass and metal tables holding ash trays and magazines. Purple and salmon petunias
edged the terrace and beyond was a strip of lawn, then
a driveway, another strip of lawn reaching to the long
rose bed, and, behind it a high and straggly privet
hedge. Beyond that were two tall pine trees, their needles
glittering in the sunlight. There were also apple trees
and among them one could glimpse the Murrays' house,
not new, flat-roofed and modern like the Barrows' ranch-
type one, but a two-story and attic, rather sprawling,
rather shabby, brown-shingled house with a big porch,
a wisteria vine over it and a comfortable, flat hammock
on the porch.

Janey Murray who had lived there during her fourteen
years and five months was baby-sitting here next door at
the Barrows. All this lovely Saturday afternoon she had

been taking care of Darlene Barrow who was seven, and spoiled. It had been a long and exhausting three hours because Darlene was a child who expected to be played with every minute. Paper dolls which had bored her strewed the terrace and a princess paper doll had blown into the petunia border where she stood with a silly smile, dressed in a slip and knee-deep in blossoms. Snips and strips of paper had blown onto the lawn. The elder Barrows, when they came back from swimming in the Prospect Hill Club pool would not be pleased to find papers all over the place, not pleased at all. Nor would they be pleased, Janey thought, unhappily, if Darlene kept on refusing to eat her supper.

The child, dressed in a very frilly, sticking-out style dress, sat at a glass table swinging her legs, holding her lips tightly shut, making faces, shaking her head until the little blond pony-tail flipped wildly this way and that. Janey had made peanut-butter sandwiches for her, jelly sandwiches, bread and honey, cinnamon toast, a scrambled egg and had offered her crunchy, well-sugared cereals. "I hate that, I hate that, I hate that," Darlene had managed to chant between clenched teeth. She was fat and pretty and maddening. Her parents worried about her, thinking she would wither and blow away if she ever missed even half a meal.

Janey stood by the table looking down at her, worn out and at her wits' end. She held a glass saucer with some canned cherries in it, put this down on the table and said, "Here, try these. Did you ever hear the story of the fisherman who was eating a cherry? He threw the pit behind him and by mistake it hit a huge invisible demon and the demon was furious. . . ."

"Where was the fisherman?" Darlene asked. "Was he fishing near my grandmother's island in the Sound?"

Her grandmother, Mrs. Barrow, Senior, owned an island with a lovely old house on one of the Thimble Islands in Long Island Sound. This was Three Pines Island about a mile offshore and some ten or fifteen miles east of New Haven, the city where the Barrows and the Murrays lived.

Janey said, "This story was about an Arabian fisherman. I don't believe there are any invisible demons around the Connecticut shores." To her great relief, Darlene had picked up her spoon and put a cherry in her mouth. Janey dropped down into a long chair and closed her eyes.

Darlene began to count the cherries, half-singing, "Rich man, poor man, beggar man, thief. . . ."

Janey lay still, relaxing, thinking how much she would have liked to spend the afternoon in the Prospect Hill Club pool, but her father, Matthew Murray, didn't belong because he was not a rich man. Which was why Janey spent all her free time baby-sitting. Sometimes at night before she went to sleep she would think how utterly marvelous it would be to write a best-seller novel or a play that was a Broadway hit, or even to dive into deep water and find a chest of gold that had been pirates' treasure. There used to be pirates in Long Island Sound. Then she would have the most wonderful time thinking of what she would buy with the money: clothes for herself and her young brother and sister Jimmy and May. They were at a late summer camp now in New Hampshire. And she would buy a new car and a new roof, for the house leaked in one corner of the kitchen. It would be nice to have a permanent because her dark hair was so straggly when she let it out of her pony-tail, and she knew that wasn't becoming. Perhaps she pulled it back too tightly and that gave her sort of a skinned look. If she ever had really plenty of money, she'd buy one of these huge round rubber swimming pools for the garden. She so loved swimming. But perhaps it would be more important for her future to take a beauty course at one of these charm schools. She wondered how much it would cost to take a course in *How to be Popular*.

She lay thinking, in the long chair with her hands under the back of her head, when Darlene said, "Tell me the story about the fisherman and the cherry pit. What did the invisible mad demon do?"

What did he do? Janey couldn't remember. She was relieved when at that moment a car came up the driveway: a long, smoothly polished gray town car, with four doors. It stopped, a door opened and slammed. A tall, red-headed boy of sixteen or seventeen had got out.

Darlene turned and rudely spat out a cherry pit at him as he took long steps to the terrace. He dodged the pit and said, "Hi, Darlene darlin'. Are your parents home?" His accent was just slightly Irish. He nodded at Janey. She thought he looked worried.

She sat up on the foot rest of her chair and explained about the Barrows and the pool. "They should be back any minute now," she said. "I'm Jane Murray from next door, baby-sitting."

"I'm Patrick McGill," he replied and stood, looking troubled, rubbing his left hand up and down through the back of his crew-cut hair. He had long arms and legs, a thin, tanned face and a wide mouth. He was a friendly looking boy, she thought, and liked him.

She had heard the Barrows talking about him before he came to visit his grandmother. There had been all kinds of wild tales. The Barrows were his mother's family, and they had never seen the boy before and really knew almost nothing about him. His father had always been sort of a rolling stone of an Irishman. It was thought that he made more or less of a living by selling bottled lemon-ade, called lemon-squash. Some of them thought he sold it in a little grocery store he owned somewhere in mid-Ireland in a town on the Shannon River. Some of the Barrows thought he drove around with a donkey and a cart peddling the bottles of lemon-squash. Nobody could quite understand how he happened to be down in Florida when he died in the summer, but Pat had had to come up to his grandmother, Mrs. Barrow, Senior, a month ago. His relatives in this house, Janey thought, did try not to be ashamed of him. They didn't really mean to be un-kind.

Darlene, staring at him now, was not being polite or tactful. She always liked to point out the faults in boys and girls older than herself. She said, as if she had been his elderly aunt instead of a much younger cousin, "Pat, you've got on a raggedy jacket and a patch on your pants and you shouldn't stick a magazine in your pocket. He's our new cousin," she explained to Janey. "He's stay-ing with our grandmother on Three Pines Island. Pat, you've got big holes in your socks."

He said, but not disagreeably, "You've got big holes in your manners, Miss Darlene, and that's worse than holes in socks. You should be mending your manners. Do you think I could reach my uncle, Mr. Barrow, if I telephone the club?" he asked Janey.

She said she thought he might but that probably the family were on their way home.

Darlene was accusing Pat loudly, "You've been driving my grandmother's car, Pat McGill! You're not supposed to touch it."

"There was an emergency," the boy said. "I'll go in and telephone."

As he stepped toward the door to the house another car drove up; a station wagon, the colors of cream and coffee and sugar, longer, richer, smoother even than the gray car. A proud tan poodle and five Barrows got out: Darlene's parents, her sister Kit, aged sixteen, her brother Ronnie, seventeen, and her brother Willie who was eight. Janey often felt that this family, their house, their furniture, stove, refrigerator and cars all looked as if they had just been cut out of the advertisements of some extremely expensive magazine.

Mr. Barrow said, "Hi, everybody!" He was fat, older than his wife, red-faced, gray-haired. He said, "Hi, Patrick, is your grandmother here?"

The boy answered, "Well, not exactly here. You see—"

Darlene interrupted, banging her spoon on the rim of her glass saucer and shouting out, "Why didn't you take me? I've had a perfectly horrible afternoon. I wanted to go swimming. I'm always left out of everything!"

Her mother said, "Darling, you won't be allowed in the club pool until you're four feet tall."

The child wept loudly, "I don't want four feet. I'm not a dog."

Everybody laughed. Her father picked her up and kissed her. He asked her who was his baby, said she was a living doll and kissed her again.

"Is grandmother in the house?" Mrs. Barrow asked Pat, as if just remembering.

"She's not, I'm afraid, Aunt Cindy," he answered. "You see, around two o'clock she didn't feel too well so she called up the doctor and he told her to come in to New Haven, and, you see, the Goodwards are off for the day." The Goodwards were Mrs. Barrow, Senior's, couple who lived with her on the island and worked for her. "So since they weren't there," Pat explained, "she wanted me to row her ashore. The Goodwards had taken the motor-boat. So I rowed her ashore and got her car out of the garage on Green Cove, and drove her in."

"But where is your grandmother?" Mr. Barrow asked anxiously, and told Darlene not to choke him to death. He was still holding her and she was hugging his neck so tightly he was turning purple.

Pat went on, rather unhappily, "Well, I took her to the doctor's and parked nearby and waited and then after a time the nurse came out and said the doctor wanted her to go right to the hospital and was arranging for a room and everything. So I took her there, and then came out here. I did try twice to telephone you, Uncle Will, but the line was busy each time."

Mrs. Barrow said, "One of you children must have left the receiver off the hook."

They all said they hadn't, but Janey thought they probably had. It often happened. She was going about now picking up bits of paper, and she was sorry to see that Pat seemed so troubled and that everyone's attitude was that it had all been his fault.

"Well, good gracious," Mr. Barrow said, "I'll go in and telephone the hospital and the doctor and find out what the score is. Here, baby, stand on your own feet." He put Darlene down and hurried into the house.

Mrs. Barrow stood looking at Pat, frowning and twisting up one of the little curls of fair hair at the back of her neck. She said, "My dear Pat, now what can we do with you? You shouldn't be on the island without your grandmother, should you? I mean there was that account in the paper a few days ago about vandals or water pirates breaking into two houses on the Thimble Islands. I wouldn't like to think of your being there without her, since the Goodwards sleep in their apartment over the boathouse."

Pat grinned and said, "Well now, Aunt Cindy. I had it in the back of my mind that I was there to protect my grandmother. I wouldn't be expecting a woman over seventy to pick up her poker and run downstairs and bang three or four vandals over the head while I shivered behind her—that is, if any marauders did land on the island and break into the house. I doubt if they'd take the trouble."

This seemed to annoy his relatives. They said, more or less at once, that his grandmother had a lot of valuable things in that house: the silver bowls and the silver tea set, the three pieces of Lowestoft china and the small Pierce portrait and the Currier and Ives winter scene.

"Not to mention the gilt buttons of George Washington," Kit, Darlene's sister, said. She was in a long chair, relaxing, looking beautiful in a crisp candy-striped dress.

Janey envied her. She herself felt disheveled. At one point in the long, hard afternoon Darlene had insisted that Janey pretend to be a pony and she the rider. This sport had not been too good for Janey's rather old blue cotton dress. She sat down on the edge of the terrace now with the paper dolls and their dresses and a lot of snips of paper in her lap.

On the terrace Ronnie also was stretched out in a long chair and had picked up a magazine. The poodle lay in the sun in the petunia bed. Mrs. Barrow was straightening Darlene's hair. Willie had torn a page out of one of the magazines and was making a paper dart. Patrick McGill half sat on the edge of a table.

He said, "What is it about George Washington's gilt buttons? Just before she was taken sick grandmother had asked me if sometime I'd make a search for them and I didn't understand."

From behind his magazine, Ronnie said, "Those buttons are supposed to be the hidden treasure of the Barrows."

"The great Barrow mystery," Kit added, laughed and also took up a magazine.

Their mother explained, as if half her thoughts were elsewhere, that a very old cousin had once given the children's grandfather's grandfather six or perhaps more gilt buttons and said they had belonged to George Washington. Nobody ever knew whether they really had been his, or had just belonged to some slave, or anybody. No one in this family had ever seen them. Mrs. Barrow, Senior, remembered them vaguely and thought that years before she had put them away for safekeeping somewhere in the Three Pines Island house, but had no idea where.

"The point now is," Kit said, turning over a page of her magazine, "that people are getting all steamed up over buttons because of that man who spoke on the T.V. program about collections three weeks ago."

"Button collections!" Ronnie muttered scornfully.

Mrs. Barrow finished with Darlene's pony-tail and kissed her. She said, "Now, honey-pie, you look sweet. Really button collections are interesting, darlings, and the rare ones are worth a great deal." She went on to say that if you had a George Washington inaugural button you might get anywhere from ten to one hundred and fifty dollars for it, and that if the six gilt ones were really his they would be worth a fabulous amount. A man who wrote a book about buttons said there had been gilt ones on the brown broadcloth suit Washington had worn for his inauguration ceremonies in New York, and these had been lost. "Sometime we'll have to organize a search and hunt all through grandmother's house on the island," Mrs. Barrow said.

Kit yawned and said it would surely be completely superlative if they could find and sell them. They could go on a Caribbean cruise with the money. "Or spend a month skiing at Sun Valley this winter," Ronnie suggested. "Or build a fully equipped rocket workshop and laboratory in the back garden," Willie shouted. He launched his paper dart, perhaps not intentionally at Janey, but it hit her in the ear.

Pat, looking at him angrily, said, "Watch out where you aim your missiles, you young ruffian."

But Willie laughed and started to make another dart.

Mr. Barrow came out of the house then, said he had been talking to his mother's nurse and that all was under control. His mother had been given a sedative and was sleeping at present. "Still I think we'd better drive right down, Cindy," he said to his wife, "and see if everything is okay. Now about you, my boy," he said to Pat. "Will you stay here with us until your grandmother can go back to the island—or what?"

Janey knew it would be most inconvenient for the William Barrows to have Pat spend even one night here. In spite of its size, this was only a three bedroom house. Ronnie and young Will shared a room so where would Pat sleep? Perhaps downstairs in the rumpus room on a couch.

He was saying, "Well thanks, Uncle Will, but I think I'd better be going back to the island myself. I'm afraid we left some of the windows open and if it storms it'll rain in, and also maybe I should be there to protect the gilt buttons, if there are water pirates around."

Janey thought he was teasing his relatives a little, but they didn't realize it.

Mr. Barrow, sounding relieved, said that perhaps this was the best plan and admonished him to drive out carefully.

"I am not sure that I should drive at all, sir," Pat answered. "The car didn't steer properly coming in. She would pull toward the left and shiver. I think it should be checked, sir."

Mr. Barrow and Ronnie said quickly and somewhat crossly that, of course, it should be checked, that it mustn't be driven a block until a mechanic went over it. Then the question came up of how Pat was to get back to Green Cove. Nobody offered to drive him in another car. He still half sat on the edge of the table swinging one long leg and not only was there a hole in his sock but also in his dirty white sneaker.

Poor Patrick, Janey thought, it must be hard to be a relative of the perfect Barrows.

The boy was saying, "I'd better take the bus out."

"You poor kid." Kit didn't look up from her reading. "There won't be a bus for those shore towns for an hour and it'll take another hour to Green Cove, the route winds around so."

"And then that long row out to the island!" Mrs. Barrow also was sympathetic. "You won't get there until after dark."

But still nobody offered to drive him. Either Mr. or Mrs. Barrow or Ronnie could perfectly well. Janey felt indignant. She was still sitting on the edge of the terrace, and was straightening the paper dolls and their clothes.

Kit suddenly remembered her and said, "Dad you owe Janey a fortune for sitting with Darlene all afternoon."

"She ought to think it's a—a treat," Darlene said pertly and was laughed at.

Kit said, "Don't be so uncouth and primitive, Darlene."

Mr. Barrow apologized and said, "Here you are, young lady," and Janey got up, put the papers on a table and went over to him. "What is it now?" he was saying. "Seventy-five an hour, about three hours, three fives are fifteen, three sevens twenty-one and add the one, is twenty-two." He was counting out money. "Two twenty-five; here you are, Janey; we appreciate it."

She thanked him and took the money, trying not to feel embarrassed, for why should she? It was a straightforward business arrangement. She looked at the boy from Ireland and said, "Good-by, Pat."

"I'll walk you home, Janey," he said.

She thought: This is the first time in all my life a boy has said he'd walk me home, and she said, aloud, "But I live just beyond the hedge."

"Ah, some wild bull might be roaming around loose up Maple Street and come at you between here and the hedge. I'd not like you to be running any risks now," he said.

His relatives obviously didn't know how to take this. Ronnie said, "Wild bulls on Maple Street!" in scorn. Mrs. Barrow, sounding a little stiff, explained that although they doubtless often had that sort of emergency in Ireland, it would never be apt to happen here.

Everybody said good-by, or "I'll be seeing you," with some constraint. Janey and Pat walked across the strip of lawn, between the two cars parked on the driveway and across the rest of the lawn to the rose border and the hedge.

As they went through the opening in it, Kit's voice came to them too clearly saying, "Can't somebody do something about his clothes? There are actually holes in the cuffs of that old gray turtle-necked sweater of his. His tweed jacket is all frayed. And his flannel slacks look as if he'd picked them up at the Salvation Army!"

She was hushed quickly, and as Janey and Pat emerged onto the Murrays' grass, the voices on the Barrows' terrace seemed far away.

Janey felt that she was bright red with anger. She said, "Don't pay any attention to them. The Barrows absolutely scorn everything unless its absolutely new and expensive: new clothes, new houses, cars, wall-to-wall carpeting, stoves and refrigerators and deep freezes. They don't think anything or anyone is any good at all unless it's worth a million dollars."

Pat said soberly, "Well, I don't wear my price tag danglin' out. And my father used to say, 'Don't be always worrying your head about what people think and say about you.' A fine, grand man he was."

"I'm sure he was," Janey agreed. They were going up the piazza steps now, and Janey thought Pat looked lonely and hungry. She remembered that the Irish liked tea, and nobody had thought about his supper. He would have the long bus ride to Green Cove, and then the row out to the island. It would be late when he reached the big dark house with nobody there, and nothing cooked and hot for him to eat. It seemed dreadfully dreary. She said, "I think you have time before your bus goes. Come in and have some tea and English muffins. I'll toast them quickly."

The loneliness went out of his brown eyes and he grinned. "Now that's the nicest thing I've heard in weeks," he said, and let the screen door slam as he followed her into the house.

2

They sat in the Murrays' kitchen, a nice, large kitchen with a gas stove, an old-fashioned built-in china cabinet, a sink whose faucet dripped, a "breakfast nook" with benches each side of a table, and on a wall a large calendar with a picture of a boy and girl gay, red-cheeked, skiing down a steep snowy mountain side. There was a rocking chair near the stove, and in the chair on a red cushion lay a black cat. Late sunlight came in through high windows over the sink where red geraniums in brown pots stood on the sill. There was a smell of tea and toasted muffins. Pat, sitting opposite Janey in the breakfast nook, spread honey on a muffin and ate as if he had not had a meal today.

They had tea in blue and white cups. Milk and sugar were in a small silver pitcher and a silver bowl. The teapot was a jolly looking fat one, brown glazed, sprinkled with tiny disks of colored glass like candies.

Janey spread her muffin with butter and said in a worried tone, "If you're going to be alone in that big house on Three Pines Island, I do hope no vandals go there to-night."

"Ah, they won't," he answered. "All that talk is non-sense, just sparrows' chatter."

"But would thieves, I mean water pirates, try to steal the George Washington buttons?"

"How could they ever know that maybe my grand-mother had any?" the boy asked. "I mean, if she didn't even remember much about them herself and couldn't remember where she hid them."

Janey said, "People in the country seem to know every-thing about each other. I think I've heard that your grandmother has been going to that house on Three Pines Island for fifty years. Probably everybody in Green Cove and the other little towns along on the shore knows all about what she has and about everything that happens to her!"

"I'm sure it's true," he agreed. "It's the same in Ire-land. Why, surely every man and woman and child in the village used to know what my father and I were going to do next, or where we were going to travel before he and I knew it or had decided it ourselves. It's probably the same here. Maybe there are ten old women in Green Cove who know where she hid the George Washington buttons while she herself has forgotten entirely." He bit his muffin, chewed and swallowed it with evident enjoy-ment.

"Have you been over here long?" she asked and spread honey on her own muffin.

"In this country since late last winter," he told her. "My father had this fishing shack in Florida on Lemon Key and we thought he might get rid of a bad cold he'd picked up in Dublin. It's very cold and damp there in winter, you know." His voice was becoming sadder as was the expression in his eyes. He said, "Well, we flew over in March and at first my father seemed to be getting better and I had skin-diving lessons with a group of boys in a place called Marathon. It was good for awhile, I can tell you, but after two months—" He stopped as if he couldn't go on, but then he did, and pushed crumbs around into patterns on the table. "You see, I could rent an aqua-lung there and the water was as clean and clear as glass. It was keen, as the guys say here. It was really keen, and some of father's friends used to come down to Lemon Key from the north to see him. But after three months. . . ." He stopped and when, after a moment or two, he went on, his voice was toneless. "Well, he got worse and he died in July and then my guardian, one of his friends, Dan Owens, got in touch with my mother's family the Barrows and my grandmother wrote that I was to fly up to her on Three Pines Island. So that's what I did."

Janey poured more tea for him out of the fat teapot, and asked, "You've never known your mother's family well?"

From a full spoon he dripped honey onto another half muffin and explained that he'd spent his life in Ireland or England or on the continent and that anyway there'd been a sort of misunderstanding, almost a feud between his father and the Barrows. His mother Nancy had been the only girl in a family of five older brothers. They and Nancy's father hadn't wanted her to marry Peter McGill. The Barrows all had a fierce prejudice against the Irish. It was a pity, but there it was.

The black cat in the rocking chair woke up, flexed its claws, jumped down to the floor, stretched, came over to the table and rubbed itself against Pat's leg, purring. He put his hand down and scratched it behind the ears.

Pat said, "You see, my mother and father eloped and her family never forgave them. My mother died when I was four—"

"Mine died when I was eight," she said, softly.

"Ah, I'm sorry. That makes us alike." His voice and the expression of his face showed his sympathy.

She said, "And I have a nice grandmother too, but she's one of the thin, not very old, ones who is always traveling around the world. Now and then she remembers us and drops down out of the clouds to buy us some clothes and to see if we keep our voices pitched low and are speaking properly. She says it's frightfully important." She broke off and asked, "Who took care of you after your mother died, Pat?"

"My father himself and a good old housekeeper, Mrs. Nolan."

"We have a housekeeper, Mrs. Kenney, but she's at a niece's wedding this afternoon."

He smiled and said housekeepers always had masses of nieces and nephews who were always getting married, and here he and Janey were alike on another point. He took another swallow of tea and said, "Do you like living here in a house that's one of a lot of houses along a straight street? I—well I've always lived with more space around me. Do you like it?"

She realized that nobody had ever asked her before if she liked living on Maple Street. Perhaps she had never even asked herself. She had a muffin halfway to her mouth and she said, "You know sometimes I like it and sometimes I'm absolutely *desperate* wanting something exciting to happen. I simply long to go somewhere where I could climb high snow mountains or explore hidden Aztec cities, or hunt big game in Africa and bring back a lion cub for a pet."

He said, "Now that would be fun, wouldn't it! Imagine leading a lion cub along Maple Street! I'd like to see all the good housewives squeal and run and drop their supermarket bundles on the sidewalk while they went scampering into the house and locked their doors."

"And the lion cub ate up the hamburger meat and the rolls and the butter that they dropped."

The two looked at each other and laughed.

"Don't you sometimes feel that you absolutely long and *yearn* to have something exciting happen?" she said.

"Do I ever not," he agreed.

"But you don't have this everlasting helping the housekeeper with cooking and vacuum cleaning, and taking dishes and silver out of the dish washer and putting them away, and setting the table, and being nice to your little brother and sister when they're not at camp. Even though you do love them awfully, sometimes it gets tiresome. And having to make money to help your father, by everlasting baby-sitting, baby-sitting, baby-sitting! I like kids, but—"

"But you'd like a lion cub for a change." He nodded, laughed and got up. "I can imagine just how you feel," he said. "Look, I really have to go. Would it be all right if I telephoned for a taxi?"

"Of course," she answered. "It's in the pantry—the telephone, I mean, not the taxi. Look, Pat, you aren't going to take a taxi all the way out to Green Cove? It'll cost a fortune."

"Not out to the cove, just into the center of town where I can pick up the bus for the shore places." He went out of the room followed by the cat Ebon who held her tail high.

Janey got up, cut more muffins and put the two halves into the toaster. She heard Pat in the pantry dialing his number. She thought it was extravagant for him to be taking a taxi anywhere, but what a nice boy he was and how easy to talk to him. Usually she had a hard time thinking up anything to say to boys and that, she knew, was one reason why she was never popular.

She looked at the wall clock and realized that her father would be home soon from his office downtown in the college building. She must get supper for him, soup perhaps and a salad; and Mrs. Kenney had left some pudding in the icebox. She got up to take things out.

Pat came back just as the muffin halves jumped up out of the toaster and flung themselves onto the table. He said he was always fascinated by these gadgets, and sat fussing with the toaster.

Washing lettuce at the sink, Janey said she was sorry he would have such a long bus ride back.

"Oh, it doesn't matter," he said. "I have my skin-diving magazine and I'll read that on the way." He patted his pocket where a magazine protruded. "I passed all my tests in Florida," he said, "and now all I need for real Scuba work is an aqua-lung of my own. Some way or other I've got to scrape enough money together to buy my own lung."

She recognized the importance of this, knew from his

tone and the seriousness of his expression that this was the one great, overwhelming desire of his life. "How much are lungs?" she asked.

"Oh, a million dollars."

"A million!"

"Well, for me it might as well be a million. Actually, including the regulator, they're anywhere between eighty and two hundred bucks." He was buttering another muffin.

"Couldn't you make that in any way?"

"That's what my guardian Dan Owens is always telling me I should do. He's one of these financial guys on Wall Street. He wants me to have business initiative and to learn how to make and handle money and invest it wisely. Every now and then he sends me the Wall Street Journal and I plough through it. It's not my line; at least, now it isn't. Maybe I'll become a big wheel of the financial district when I'm older. Seems dull doesn't it?" He sighed. "Awfully dull when you think of everything that's lying around under water waiting to be found; sunken Spanish ships off Florida, and sunken Greek ships in the Adriatic, not to mention the sea life and jelly fish all over the world. I've been making something of a study of jelly fish."

She said, sympathetically, "Those sound a lot more interesting than stocks and bonds and things. I think you're a little young for the Wall Street Journal. My father teaches at Yale and writes books on the financial problems of nations and I can't understand five words in them." She sometimes thought that, although her father might know all about the finances of nations, he didn't get nearly enough financial reward himself.

"But, Pat," she suggested, "couldn't you make money with a paper route or something? Our paper boy told me he makes twelve dollars a week."

"He's rolling in wealth," Pat said. "I had no idea they made so much." He sat thinking about it and then said he didn't see how he could carry on any such business enterprise because next week he was going to boarding school, St. Ronan's in Jefferson, Connecticut, up in the hills. He supposed he was lucky they would take him at all because he hadn't had much education and he couldn't get the hang of these intelligence tests they gave for entrance examinations. According to the results, he didn't have the intelligence of a three-year-old. However, the school said they'd try him. He hadn't been able to go to school regularly ever because he'd traveled about so much with his father. They'd had bits of property and little old villas here and there in Europe. He spoke vaguely, giving the impression that his father had been interested in real estate, picking up small run-down houses, selling them, probably at a loss.

A car horn outside announced that the taxi was waiting impatiently.

"This has been wonderful," Pat said. "It's as if I had been home."

Seldom had anyone said anything so warm and appreciative to Janey. It was as if she had been given the most delightful present. It was hard to know the right answer, but she said, "It's been lovely to have you."

She walked with him through the pantry and the rubbers' and galoshes' passageway, across the hall and out to the taxi, saying she hoped his grandmother would be better tomorrow, that she hoped it wouldn't be awfully late when he reached Three Pines Island, and then she added, "And I do hope you won't be bothered by water pirates coming after the Washington buttons."

He laughed and said, as he got into the taxi, "Ah surely, I think those buttons are a myth."

As the taxi started off Janey saw her father's car coming up Maple Street. It was robin's egg blue, small and six years old. Janey knew that the Barrows felt embarrassed for her whenever they caught sight of it but it was a good little car and the Murrays were attached to it. Now she waited while it came up and stopped. She felt a pleasant, warm happiness that her father was home. His long, brown-trousered legs and then the rest of him came out of the door. He was a tall, thin man, not handsome as all men are in advertisements, for instance, but he was kind and intelligent-looking. He had glasses and thick steel-gray hair and a nose with a slight bump at the right side where the bone had been broken by a baseball years before.

Now he smiled at Janey and said, "How's everything, Pet? Help me out with a board, will you? I've picked up a beautiful bit of walnut for my new bench."

He had several power tools and a workshop in the cellar and his hobby was the making of good, firm, stools and benches along early American lines. He was able to sell his furniture through a craft shop in Hartford and he always gave his children half the money from these sales and let them buy with it anything they wanted. He himself never used his share for dull necessities like shoes and spinach. "Fun money," the Murrays called it and did everything they could to encourage his working hard on the stools and benches. In fact, they thought it would be a good plan if he gave up teaching and writing and lecturing on such boring matters as international finance and devoted all his time to making things so beautifully with wood.

Now Janey helped him extricate a long board from the car. It was so awkward that they finally had to ease it through one of the windows.

"Who was the nice-looking boy who went off in the taxi?" he asked. He stood on the sidewalk holding the board on end, smoothing it with one hand absent-mindedly but as if he liked the feeling of it.

"He's Patrick McGill, the Barrows' cousin from Ireland," she answered.

"Ah, Nancy Barrow's son." Mr. Murray looked as if he were remembering something pleasant. "Nancy was quite a winner. Not up to your mother, Janey, but a good second." He picked up the board and started toward the house.

"You knew her, father?" Janey was surprised.

"I did, indeed. I danced four dances with Nancy at the Yale Prom my junior year. The man she came with wanted to shoot me at dawn, I remember." He laughed. "She wore a green dress, fluffy, really something. She married an Irishman eventually, didn't she?"

"Yes. Her brothers didn't like him."

"Ah well. There are plenty of people the Barrow brothers didn't like, your father included. However, I don't grudge them their opinions. And any son of Nancy Barrow would be a fine lad. Have you ever been out to the old lady's house on Three Pines Island, Janey?" They were going into the front hall together.

"Once in the spring. Don't you remember Kit invited

me out for the day? It's a wonderful place and the swimming was marvelous."

He said, regretfully, "I wish I could give you children an island in the Sound, and as gay a life as Barrow gives his children."

She was afraid he was going to sink into one of his gloomy moods when he sat and worried about her and her younger brother and sister and felt badly because he hadn't money enough to give them glamorous presents and clothes and gaieties.

"We have a lovely life, father," Janey told him, putting her hands on his shoulders and kissed him by the left eye.

"Well, you're a darling," he answered and kissed the top of her head. "What do you know, I've got an order for four benches from a man in Litchfield. Can't wait to get at them. Call me when supper's ready."

He opened the door from the rubbers' passageway and went on down the cellar steps. Presently, while Janey was boiling eggs to stuff for salad, the house was filled with the agreeable humming and buzzing from her father's workshop below.

As she went about the kitchen getting supper, she wondered if she would ever see Pat McGill again, really talk to him. She was troubled though about his clothes. Perhaps other people, particularly boys at boarding school, wouldn't realize what a nice, rather wonderful person he was. She hoped that his grandmother or his aunt or someone would get him a good sports jacket and new slacks before he went off to St. Ronan's. People at schools could be cruel about a person's appearance, she knew that very well. She and her young brother Jimmie and her sister May went to a Catholic school where all the girls wore similar dresses, and the boys white shirts and blue trousers. But Kit and even Darlene Barrow and, of course, Ronnie and Willie too were always buying new and very expensive clothes for school.

Moreover, Pat had a way of talking that was different and a sense of humor that wasn't like that of anyone else. She thought there was something a little mysterious about him. It wasn't too pleasant to think of his being all alone out on Three Pines Island tonight, after those accounts in the newspaper about water vandals. When she had been to the Barrows' island that day with Kit she had felt that it was very remote. It would not be a good thing if water pirates should come there by any chance tonight.

3

When Patrick McGill reached Green Cove it was dusk and a storm seemed to be rising over the water. He knocked at Ben Green's door, and the man came limping out with his right foot in a cast and bandage. He had broken it two weeks before. He was a short man with thin gray hair and a pleasant geniality. His family had owned Green Cove since Revolutionary times and from his dock and front door you looked out across the water to the Thimble Islands in the Sound. Since it was late in the season, most of the houses were closed now and boarded up but here and there a few families remained in their summer places. Some lights showed, but there was no light on Three Pines Island, the one furthest out from shore.

Mr. Green smiled when he saw Patrick, invited him to come in, and asked how his grandmother was. Mrs. Barrow, Senior, rented part of Mr. Green's old barn where she kept her car and where there was space too for Patrick's little old foreign one. There was also an arrangement with Mr. Green about his dock. Mrs. Barrow left her boats tied here when she was brought over from the island.

Patrick explained now that his grandmother was in the hospital, which news greatly shocked and distressed Mr. Green, who said he would call up at once to find out how she was.

"She didn't seem too worried about herself," Pat said, "and she was sleeping comfortably when my uncle telephoned. Still I think I'll telephone too when I get to the island. I think I'd better be starting before the storm breaks."

"It looks bad," Mr. Green said, "and there are no lights out there. Where's that couple that works for your grandma? The Goodwards? If they're off the island, why didn't they bring in the Conch Shell and leave it here?"

The Conch Shell was the name of Mrs. Barrow's twenty-two-foot motorboat.

"I think they took it down to the Branford dock and took the bus into town from there," Patrick explained.

"I don't like your rowing way out there alone late as it is," Mr. Green said. "Why not spend the night with Mrs. Green and my mother and me? We'd like to have you."

"It's good of you," Patrick answered. "I appreciate it, but we left some windows open and things'll be soaked and ruined if it rains in." He said good night and went on down to the dock.

In a few minutes he was approaching the entrance to the cove, rowing against the wind and against waves that were higher than he had expected. On shore he saw the forms of trees, of Mr. Green's barn and house. The front door was open and against a rectangle of light a man's figure stood and waved at him. There's no reason in the world for him to be worrying, Pat thought, and pulled strongly. A wave thudded against the starboard side of the boat toward the bow and broke splashing high, drenching him. Water ran down the back of his neck, which he disliked.

There was thunder in the distance, the wind was rising and darkness closing down so that it was not easy to locate rocks, and when he neared an island it was hard to distinguish its contours and tell what was shadow and what land. Since there was no light on Three Pines Island he was afraid that he might land on the wrong one. It would be dreary to go rowing around in the wind and the rain all night.

He thought of hot tea and crisp English muffins and honey. How pleasant that had been in the Murrays' kitchen, and what a nice girl Janey Murray was! He liked her better than any girl he'd met in this country. He'd never seemed to be able to talk to a girl before.

Hot tea and English muffins! Well, he could make himself tea and toast at least if he ever reached the island! It was surely a long, hard trial of effort. The wind seemed to be trying to push his boat around and he had to fight it with all his strength. It was almost dark now and there came another roll of thunder and a crack of lightning. Furthermore, the boat seemed to be leaking and his feet were soaked. He looked over his left shoulder and saw rather far off two low black rocks he thought he recognized. There was very rough water beyond them; white caps indicating, he thought, the tumultuous stretch of water known as the Styx Channel. Yes, there beyond it he could make out the sandy bar with a small hill. Bay-

• 31 •

berry Bush Island, about as large in area as his grand-mother's living and dining room combined. Now he knew where he was. Three Pines Island was, roughly, a quarter of a mile toward the northeast of the Styx Channel. Now, toward the right, he recognized his grandmother's island. Putting more effort into rowing, it was not long before he came into the quieter water in the lea of her shore, pulled up to her dock, fastened the line around a piling and got out, carrying the oars.

The boathouse where the launch and sailboat were kept was some fifty yards along the beach. There was no light in the Goodwards' rooms so he knew they had not re-turned from their afternoon off.

Trees dripped on his head, pine needles were slip-pery beneath his feet and bushes were wet against him as he walked up the steep path. There was a smell of bay-berry and pine, of rain and salt water and wild roses. The house was a big bulk ahead in darkness. He went up wide porch steps, put down the oars and walked across to the front door which he found unlocked. Peo-ple seldom locked anything on the Thimble Islands. When Patrick had come here in July his grandmother had once said to him, "Lock the doors? Good gracious, do you think the squirrels and the rabbits would come in and steal the silver? We haven't had a robbery on the Thimbles in all the fifty years I've lived here." But he thought now of the water pirates who had been around recently.

The door squeaked as Patrick opened it. A clock ticked. There was a rustling of a mouse or squirrel in the walls. When Patrick pushed up an electric switch button no light responded. He made his way across the wide hall to the living room and found that the lights were out there as well. His grandmother had her own generating system on the island. It was often out of order and must be now. This was a bother because the water pump, the water heater, the icebox and stove all ran by electricity.

Pat was soaked, chilled and hungry. As he stood wondering if it would be worthwhile to light a fire on the hearth and boil a kettle over it as in the farm houses in Ireland there came a great crash of thunder and crackle of lightning. Wind tore through the open windows and must, he knew, be blowing in the heavy rain. He ran around in darkness, pushing screens up, pulling windows down. He stopped a moment in the front hall and felt around in the coat closet on the shelf where the flashlight should be, but none was there. Probably he himself had left it somewhere where it didn't belong. By the time he had bumped into things and managed to shut a dozen windows downstairs and up, he hadn't energy enough to go down again, build and light a fire in the living room, try to balance a teakettle on the wood and wait until it boiled. Nor did he feel like bumbling around the kitchen and in the icebox feeling for food. It wouldn't hurt him to go to bed hungry. He had done it before.

Upstairs in his own room at the west side of the house he remembered a foolish little pencil flashlight. Blindly exploring in his desk drawer he found it. The beam was pitifully weak but better than nothing. He put the small torch on the table, undressed and got into bed. Through the open window he heard wind in the trees and waves against the rocks and the shore, but the rain seemed to have stopped.

He wondered if there really were George Washington's buttons hidden somewhere in the house. There might well be. His grandmother was always forgetting where she put her glasses, for instance. He hoped she was comfortable in the hospital and would be home soon. He wished he had remembered to telephone her but was too sleepy to get up now. She was a nice person, his grandmother, but not an easy one to know well, and not easy to talk to, not in the least as Janey Murray was.

He wondered drowsily when the Goodwards would be home, and then he slept.

Pat was wakened an hour or more later by the sound of footsteps on the path, coming up onto the porch very carefully and quietly as if someone was anxious not to be heard. He sat up in bed and the wind coming in the window was chill and damp. He heard the front door squeak and wished that he had locked it, wished very much that he had and wondered what he should do.

There was no light in the Goodwards' apartment in the boathouse, no candle or lamp showing through the trees. He doubted if they were home. If they had come back the sound of the Conch Shell's motor would have wakened him, surely. He thought he was alone here on the island and that vandals or water pirates had rowed over, "with muffled oars," whatever those might be, and someone was now tiptoeing around downstairs.

They were! He heard a board creak, heard someone bump into something. He didn't know what he should do, but he did know that he wasn't going to hide up here and let anyone make off with his grandmother's silver. Of course he had no revolver, and probably they had. Unpleasant thought! Nor was it agreeable to think of going downstairs and walking straight into a situation of this kind. Part of his mind told him that sensible older men would tell him he was a fool to consider it, that he ought to lie still in bed and pretend to be asleep. But another, a rash and reckless part of his mind, kept urging him to get up and go downstairs and see what he could do about this. He could at least shout in a rough voice and order the intruders off and they might flee.

He sat up on the edge of his bed, his feet feeling for slippers. He remembered that once his father had told him that a straight chair was not a bad weapon of defense. If an enemy comes at you to strike or kick you, pick up the nearest straight chair. Hold it with the four legs sticking out in front of you and go at your opponent. Maybe you can knock him off balance. Anyway he can't get through the chair legs to bash you. This is a good trick unless he has a revolver and you haven't. Then he has it all his own way.

Pat picked up and snapped on his pencil flashlight, crossed the room and took up a straight-backed desk chair. Carrying this in his left hand, he went quietly out of the room and down the hall.

Someone was below in the living room; more than one person. He heard them moving and whispering and saw a beam of light. Looking down over the railing of the stair well, he saw a torch's light move high across the wall and rest on an oil painting of cows, then move on to a stuffed deer's head above the mantel and next go to a cabinet in which were his grandmother's collection of old jars and jugs from England and the Orient. Then the light beam dropped lower and for a moment was out of sight.

About him the house seemed enormous and he felt as if he were locked in a vast box with two unseen enemies. He clutched the chair firmly and tiptoed on along the hall and started down the stairs.

Then he heard a boy's frightened voice saying, "Gosh, I don't want to *steal* anything. I've come out here, haven't I! I took my uncle's outboard dinghy. I'm here. You're the witness."

An older boy's voice ordered, "Shut up. You've got to take along a trophy. You've got to capture a trophy to show the initiation committee, otherwise how're they going to believe you've passed the test."

Pat thought, So this is an initiation ordeal, and he was certainly glad he had boys and not men to contend with.

The older one was saying, "Here, take one of these dumb old jars, nobody'll ever miss it in a thousand years."

Pat was halfway down the stairs now. In the living room he saw a figure with a sailor's white hat on its head. The other boy held the flashlight and the beam showed the china cabinet, the white-hatted boy opening its glass door, reaching up for a jar.

Making his voice as deep and as Irish-sounding as possible, Pat shouted out, "Here, you two rapscallions get out of here!" As he started to run down the stairs, he heard a horrified gasp. Holding the chair in front of him, he stormed across the hall and into the living room.

There were the two boys—one standing by the cabinet, the other by the fireplace, who shouted, "It's just a kid." He leaned over, picked up a log from the wood basket and flung it at Pat. He hurled the chair and knocked the flashlight out of the boy's hand. Innumerable things seemed to happen at once. There was a crash of china falling to the floor and breaking. The boy by the cabinet, sounding terrified and nearly weeping, said, "Oh gosh, let's get out of here, let's get out of here *now!*" The second one kept ordering, "Get your trophy. Get your trophy."

Pat saw the flashlight rolling around on its side and making a moving pool of light on the floor. In the pool were pieces of one of his grandmother's blue and white jars, broken into fragments. The boy with the white hat was on his hands and knees scrambling about picking up bits of the jar and also a white handkerchief that he seemed to have dropped from his pocket. At least, Pat thought it was his handkerchief.

The older boy was taking up another log from the wood basket. Before he could throw it Pat jumped at him. The two clutched and tangled. The torch got kicked under a sofa. Wrestling, Pat felt that his opponent was not stronger than he. They struggled, banging into a small table, knocking it over. A lamp crashed. The boy in the white cap made for the door and fell over another table, sending it with its lamp, ash trays and magazines to the floor. It must have been a heavy ash tray used as a missile that struck Pat on the head and knocked him into unconsciousness.

It was still dark and chilly when he came to, with a bumped and aching head. He felt it and was glad that his fingers were not sticky with blood. How long he had been "out" he had no idea. It was still night. No one else was in the room and he didn't know whether or not the

Goodwards had returned. He doubted it. Probably he was still alone on the island. What he needed now was food and something hot to drink but he didn't have the energy to get it. Tea and English muffins! With difficulty he got to his feet and made his way up the stairs to bed.

4

He woke with sunlight in the room and the sound of a vacuum cleaner humming downstairs. The Goodwards must be home and the electricity on. Rubbing his hand over his head he felt a bump above his right ear but it was not bad. When he had got out of bed, he was a little dizzy but that passed while he was taking his shower.

Presently, wearing blue jeans and his thin, turtle-necked gray sweater, he went downstairs. The living room had been put to rights and Mrs. Goodward was in the kitchen washing dishes. He went through the dining room and pantry and the woman looked up at him as he stood in the doorway. She was thin, tight-lipped and grim. She grunted when he said good-morning and he was sorry to see that she was in a cross mood.

He said, "My grandmother was taken ill yesterday. I drove her in to the doctor's and the hospital."

"Mr. Green told me," she answered. "He called up an hour or more ago to see if you got home all right."

"That was kind of him," Pat said.

Mrs. Goodward made a face. She had never liked Mr. Green. Water splashed noisily in the sink. She put a saucer in the dish rack and said, with her back to Pat, "Your uncle, Mr. Barrow, telephoned awhile ago. Your grandmother's got to stay in the hospital a week or so. You're to drive in to stay at your uncle's on Maple Street."

Pat was not happy about this. He wondered where he would sleep if he was to spend the time there before school opened. He looked at Mrs. Goodward and said, "Could I have an egg and some toast and milk maybe?" He was very hungry.

"You'd better have some orange juice. I don't know how you Irish ever live to grow up never eating any vitamins."

"Ah well," he said, "we manage." He took some bread out of the bread box and Mrs. Woodward went to the refrigerator.

As she opened the door and took out eggs and butter, she said, "You certainly had yourself a time knocking things around in the living room, didn't you?"

Her tone made him feel angry, feel reluctant to explain, yet he didn't want to give any false impressions. He said, "The electricity was off and two boys got in the house."

She stood and looked at him, eggs in one hand and butter in the other. He saw from her expression that she didn't believe him. "What do you mean? Burglars here?" she demanded.

"Not exactly burglars. I think it was an initiation test. Did they steal anything?"

"Nothing's gone as far as I can see. One of your grandma's blue and white jars was broken and a couple of tables tipped over." She went to the stove and began to fry two eggs. They made a pleasant smell but he wished Mrs. Goodward were in a better humor.

He sat at the kitchen table and ate some of the bread dry. He watched the woman. She wore a blue cotton dress and a frilly yellow apron. Even her stiff back seemed to disapprove of him. She had never seemed to like him and he knew it was because he was a "foreigner." A queer reason, he thought, for a person to be disliked, but it was often so. It was so even with his Barrow relatives. But it wasn't with Janey Murray. It hadn't made one bit of difference with her.

Mrs. Goodward slapped the plate with eggs down on the table before him, and he thanked her and sprinkled on salt and pepper. He said, "If nothing was stolen I don't see why we have to tell the police." He felt that it would be a pity to get that boy who had worn the sailor hat into trouble. He had seemed so frightened, as if he wished he were anywhere in the world except on Three Pines Island.

Mrs. Goodward brought him a glass of orange juice and said, "Police! Why bother them about a broken blue jar? Still, ask your aunt and uncle about it. You tell them your story."

Her tone was certainly disagreeable.

"Well, I will tell them," he said, and drank the orange juice. He was not too fond of this canned kind. He and his father had had too many orange trees of their own with fresh fruit right off the branches.

"It looked to me," Mrs. Goodward said, "as if somebody'd been carrying on a big hunt for something valuable in the house here, somebody'd been taking advantage of being here alone."

Now he was truly angry, but his father had always been stern about losing one's temper so Pat made no reply. He supposed that Mrs. Goodward had been referring to the Washington buttons. Obviously that T.V. program about collections had revived people's interest in buttons and the neighborhood remembered the story about Mrs. Barrow's owning some historic ones.

Mrs. Goodward went toward the kitchen door and then stopped and turned toward him. She had pale yellowish hair frizzed and curled. "If you're driving to New Haven in your jalopy," she said, "perhaps you'll take my husband and me in. We're going to look for another place."

"You're leaving?" He thought it was hard on his grandmother to lose these people when she was ill.

Mrs. Goodward said it was too lonesome out here in the midst of water and nowhere. For a moment she said nothing and then burst out with, "Nobody landed on the island last night. Not a boat can touch shore here without my husband's hearing it."

"But you weren't home then," Pat said.

"We were home when you came back," she answered, angrily. "We heard you walking up from the dock." She went out of the room and if the swinging door could slam he was sure she would have slammed it.

He buttered his bread and ate his eggs. He felt that Mrs. Goodward wasn't telling the truth and wondered why. He also wondered why she had not believed him when he said that boys had come into the house last night. Perhaps it was all part of her prejudice about his being a "foreigner." The whole experience had been exciting last night but not at all an agreeable sort of excitement. He doubted if even Janey Murray would have enjoyed it.

And it would be miserable to have to spend two weeks with the Barrows—sleeping where? Perhaps on the sofa in the living room! He frowned as he finished his eggs and he wished he were in his place in Florida, the "fishing shack," or at the farm in Ireland, or at the odd little house his father had bought in Yugoslavia on the shore of the Adriatic where there was such wonderful swimming. He would far rather be here alone on the island than crowd into his uncle's household, but he felt sure they wouldn't let him stay here. They were truly conscientious about trying to do what was best for him. He appreciated it, but he doubted if he would ever hit it off well with that family. He took his dishes to the sink and began to wash them.

At least Janey Murray would be next door and that was one good thing anyway. This was the first time in his life he had thought it would be pleasant to have a girl as a friend.

It was late that afternoon and Janey Murray was baby-sitting again; not exactly sitting, but Mrs. Barrow had asked her to take Darlene to a puppet show at the museum. Janey had enjoyed it more than she expected and it had made her think that perhaps she herself might be able to make hand puppets and work up little performances. Perhaps she could do them for parties. Would fifteen dollars an afternoon be too much, she wondered? Patrick McGill would be a wonderful puppeteer she thought.

Darlene hadn't been much impressed. The ones on T.V. were much better, she said. This, she said, had been a dumb show. She liked T.V. better than "live" productions anyway, or she would if they had a color T.V. When they reached the Barrows' house on Maple Street she skipped on in ahead of Janey chanting, "I want a color T.V., a color T.V. Mary Rose Palmer has one. Why can't we?" Janey followed her through the living room out onto the terrace.

Patrick McGill was again half sitting on the edge of one of the glass-topped tables. The William Barrow family were sitting around looking at him and at a man and woman whom Janey recognized as the couple who worked for Mrs. Barrow, Senior, on Three Pines Island. She had seen them there the time in the spring when Kit Barrow had invited her out to her grandmother's for a day's swimming. These Goodwards seemed to have been accusing Patrick of something. It was as if Janey had stepped into the midst of a quarrel, a serious and frightening crisis.

Janey was about to back away into the living room again and hurry home when she saw that Patrick was looking at her. He didn't put it into words but his eyes seemed to be saying, "Don't go. Stick around a few minutes. Don't go."

Darlene began again to demand color T.V., and her father said, impatiently, "Just hold it, Baby-doll, will you please? Janey, amuse her for a few minutes, will you, until we get this sorted out?"

So Janey took up a magazine and whispered to Darlene to look at pictures with her and plan which advertisements of kitchens and laundries and bedrooms they could cut out to make a scrapbook of a house for paper dolls. They sat on the edge of the terrace with the petunia border below them. The poodle had dug up some of the plants and was lying in the dirt in the sun.

Mr. Barrow, sounding greatly worried, said, "Well, now, Pat my boy, your story is that you heard sounds downstairs and went down to investigate. You saw two intruders, ordered them off, fought with one and were knocked out cold?"

Darlene piped up, "I saw a program just like that on the Lem Coleman hour, only Lem shot one of the burglars. Did you shoot one, Pat?"

"How could I?" he answered. "I didn't have a gun, and anyway they weren't burglars. They were two boys about my age and it was an initiation stunt."

"But Pat, dear, how did you know? Did you talk with them?" his aunt asked. She too sounded dreadfully worried.

"I heard them talking," Pat replied. He was swinging his leg. The sole of his sneaker was beginning to tear away from the toe.

Ronnie Barrow, stretched out as usual in one of the long chairs, said, "But gosh, fella! It's hard to believe that anybody would be fool enough to go charging into two burglars without a gun in his hand."

"Well, I had a chair," Pat said.

Everybody looked as if they thought he was crazy.

Mrs. Goodward spoke up then, excitedly. She said, "If you ask me I think he saw the Lem Coleman show and got ideas from it. When I went over to the big house this morning it looked to me as if he'd had himself a time trying to find something that he knew was hidden around somewheres and he hadn't had a chance to hunt for before because his grandma was there in the house. It looked to me as if he was hunting for something and knocked over things and broke one of his grandma's valuable old jars and thought up this story to make it look as if burglars had been there."

Pat McGill's voice sounded very controlled but very angry, and as if it came from a man at least in his twenties. He said, "Mrs. Goodward is mistaken and prejudiced. There is no truth in her version of what happened. I do not lie."

Mr. Barrow said quickly, and miserably, "No, no, my boy. We're not suggesting that, you know. Not at all. I only want to get to the bottom of this. And I wonder if I should report it to the police."

"Why, sir, when nothing was stolen? Why take up the time of the police when it was just an initiation stunt and nothing of value was taken."

Mr. Goodward spoke up then. He was a short, bald man who seemed to leave most of the talking to his wife. But he did say, "My wife said that as far as she could see nothing seemed to be stolen. But it's well-known something valuable was hidden in that house."

"And it's my guess it was found." Mrs. Goodward's voice rose high.

Kit Barrow had been lying in her long chair. She looked at the pink finger nails of her right hand and rubbed them on the palm of her left. She said, "Buttons?"

Pat McGill stood up then. It seemed to Janey that he was taller than anyone there on the terrace. Perhaps his anger made him look so. It was amazing, she thought with admiration, that he could speak so quietly, and yet have everyone know that he was in such a rage.

He said, "Uncle Will, I did not hunt last night for anything hidden in the house on Three Pines Island. I would not steal buttons, or money, or a silver tea set or any article under the sun or the moon from any man or woman, far less from my own mother's mother. I have told you what happened. If you would rather accept the Goodwards' ungrounded suspicions rather than my truth, that is your choice. Janey, may I come over to your house and have some tea and English muffins?"

"Oh yes!" she answered and got up, feeling embarrassed beyond words, feeling that she would like to flare out in defense of Patrick, but something told her that he wouldn't like interference.

Mr. Barrow was urging Pat not to go off like this. He was sure they could still sort everything out to everybody's satisfaction. Pat mustn't think they doubted his word, but sometimes in the middle of the night one dreamed up things that weren't quite realistic, not quite the way things were happening.

Janey had jumped over the petunia border and Pat had stepped across it, following her. He stopped and turned toward his uncle. He said, "There's nothing more for me to say, sir. I was fully awake last night, not dreaming. My father used to say it never did any good to prolong unpleasant arguments; state your case truthfully and let it rest. Sir, my case rests." He made a little bow, with dignity. Then he looked down at Janey, smiled a little and said, "Girl, I'm hungry enough to eat your lion cub."

"They're dreadful!" she whispered indignantly, as they walked away. "I wanted to throw things at every one of them."

He grinned and shook his head. They had reached the hedge.

From behind them, Darlene piped up shrilly, "But he's awfully poor, and those buttons are worth hundreds and thousands. He's awfully poor and he's just crazy to buy an aqua-lung for his dumb old skin-diving!"

"Hush, Baby-doll!" Mrs. Barrow ordered her, and other voices said quickly that she must hush or he would hear.

Halfway through the hedge Pat stopped and said in a low tone, "I'm surely tempted to go back and spank that spoiled young spalpeen."

"Oh don't!" Janey begged, dreadfully afraid that he just might do it. "Come on. I have some marvelous strawberry jam and I'll toast the muffins crisp as crisp."

"Well, good then," he said. "My father used to say it was never worthwhile to waste your energy being in a fury at inferior people. And he said too there was no poison as dangerous as self-pity."

"I think your father must have been a wonderful man," Janey said, as they walked toward her house.

"Ah, he was. He was the finest man in all Ireland," and then, changing the subject, Pat asked, "And how is your lion cub today?"

Her imaginary lion cub! Pat was developing a funny sort of game from it. She said, making it up as she went along, "I'm keeping him in an old chicken-wire sort of pen out behind the garage we once kept puppies in, but he jumped over it last night and I had to chase him all down Maple Street. Old Miss Mills saw him when she was coming home from somewhere and screeched dreadfully and went tearing down the street, and her hat fell off and he stopped and ate it."

They were going up the steps to the kitchen and Pat looked down at her and laughed. "That's the way to do it," he said. "Keep the ball rolling. Keep the top spinning."

She didn't know quite what he meant, but she felt that she had cheered him up a little and was extremely glad of that.

5

They had finished their tea and were out on the Murrays' porch, sitting in the flat hammock swing, leaning back among cushions, Pat at one end and Janey at the other with a glass saucer of fudge between them.

Janey said, "I don't believe they really think you found the George Washington buttons and put them in your pocket and made off with them."

He said, soberly, frowning, "The only way I can convince them I didn't is to find them and lay them on a table in front of Uncle Will and Aunt Cindy and say, 'Here they are then. I found them this afternoon up in Grandmother's attic in an old box of hats—or skates—or a trunk of hoop skirts, or something.'" He reached out, took a piece of fudge, and bit into it. "This fudge is class A," he said. "You make it?"

She nodded and answered, "Of course, it would be simply wonderful if you could find them. I mean it would absolutely shatter the button world."

"The button world?" He laughed.

"I mean, among people who collect them. It's really a big thing, Pat. I went to the library early this morning and looked up some books on it. There were a lot of buttons made at the time of Washington's inauguration."

"Silver?"

"No, sort of coppery stuff and smooth. The initials G.W. were engraved in an oval space in the center of some of them, and 'Long Live the President' was engraved around the top half. Even these are worth a lot today."

He took another piece of fudge and said, "But are those the ones my grandmother is supposed to have?"

"I don't think so. You see the terribly valuable ones are different. They're supposed to be the ones from the coat he wore at his inauguration. It was brown cloth made near Hartford or Boston, some people think. And I read that the buttons on it were gilt, engraved with the seal of the United States."

Pat put a foot on the floor and swung the hammock, and he and Janey sat thinking. He said, "It's a long time ago, how do people know about them?"

"Miss Anderson, one of the librarians, got out these books for me. One was the real writings of George Washington. There was a letter he'd written himself the month of his inauguration. It was to Mr. Knox—"

"Who was he?" Pat interrupted.

"He was the Secretary of War and he seemed to have charge of Washington's inauguration clothes—"

"Funny job for a secretary of war," Pat interrupted again, amused.

"Yes, wasn't it. But anyway Washington wrote him

that he needed six more of the large, engraved buttons."

Pat swung higher still. He said, "Anything else about them?"

"Yes, a man named William Dunlap, who lived a hundred and fifty years ago, wrote that Washington wore these gilt buttons on his inauguration suit. Miss Anderson said that these were both 'trustworthy sources.' "

"They sound so," Pat agreed, and added, "Who said those gilt buttons were lost?"

"I read it in a book on Washington's Historical Buttons by a Mr. Abbot."

"If we are going to make a search for them, these are the first clues," Pat said.

"Yes, like finding the first mention of hidden treasure in the yellowing pages of some old diary!" She began to feel excited.

"Or coming upon an ancient map with a cross and skull and cross bones, and hills and rivers and something written in faded red ink—*Here lies treasure!*" He looked at her and grinned.

"Pat!" she said. "Wouldn't it be wonderful if we could!"

He nodded. "It would be," he answered. "How do you suppose they disappeared in the first place?"

"Oh well, perhaps when Washington had retired and was living at Mount Vernon, one day his wife was looking over their old clothes and she said, 'George, here's that suit you wore in New York when you were inaugurated. What shall I do with it? I don't want the moths to get in it. Ah, that was a great day, wasn't it! I was so proud of you standing up there on the balcony taking the oath of office, and all the crowds cheering and people crying with excitement!' "

Pat, still swinging the hammock, said quietly, "Yes, that must have been a wonderful day. I'd like to have been there. The first president of the newest nation that's come to be the greatest."

Janey took a piece of fudge and ate it, thinking. She curled her legs up under the green cotton dress and settled herself more comfortably among the cushions. She said she imagined that Mrs. Washington cut the buttons off the old brown coat and put them in her work-basket, and then after awhile some child got hold of them and played with them. Then after Martha died somebody found them and perhaps gave them around as souvenirs but probably never thought they were worth much.

"So probably they went from person to person," Pat said, "and finally they came into my grandmother's possession, that is, unless the story about them is a myth which it might well be." He stopped and looked grim and sad. "I'd hate to lose my character and my reputation just because two dishonest people accused me of stealing something that didn't exist." He began to whistle *The Wearing of the Green* in a sorrowful way.

They still swung back and forth and back and forth. Pat put his arms behind his head, and still whistled. Janey watched him. There were holes in both the elbows of his sweater and she wondered again what his Aunt Cindy would do about clothes for him for boarding school. And what about name tapes? That was a dreadful job, sewing on name tapes!

He said, "No, I can't have all the Barrow family thinking my father has a thief and a liar for a son. Janey, I've got to find those gilt buttons."

"How?" she asked. "Where?" His tone of determination made her feel excited, as if they were standing just outside the door of some adventure.

He looked at her questioningly. "How about driving out with me to Green Cove tomorrow? Early. We'll row over to Three Pines Island and I can climb up onto the piazza roof and easily get in one of the windows, and we'll explore the house. Make a thorough job of it. How about it? Are you game?"

She felt herself turning red and feeling breathless. She wanted to do it more than anything in the world. But she wondered if it was right and should she do it? She said, "Oh Pat, I'd love to. I'd simply love it. But should I, do you think? Wouldn't I be sort of a burglar?"

He said, indignantly, "You'd be my guest. It's the house of my own mother's mother. My grandmother invited me there. I have as much right in her house as anyone has. And as for looking through things, actually just about an hour before she was taken sick and had to go in to the doctor's, she told me she wished that I would make a search of the house for some buttons. How about it, Janey? Will you come with me?"

She answered, "I'll have to ask my father but I think I can, Pat. But what about your family next door? What will they say about it?"

"I'll not tell them. Or else I'll say I want to get some of my clothes I forgot and left in the closet on the island. I did, too—a decent pair of shoes, but they're too small now and make me feel as if my feet are bound the way Chinese women's used to be." He stretched out a foot in its disgraceful sneaker and they both laughed. He said, "The family next door'll be only too glad to have me off their hands for the day."

"Oh no, Pat, not really," she protested.

"I'm not bitter about them," he assured her. "They're trying hard to be nice, and sometimes the two little kids are really cute and friendly. But, after all, I realize I'm an odd fella. They think I'm sort of a zombie and naturally I make them uncomfortable."

"Where are you going to sleep while you're with them?" she asked, thinking that he was the one who was trying hard to be nice.

"In their rumpus room. It's not too bad excepting there's no window. It's air-conditioned with indirect ventilation, whatever that is. I'm used to a cold gale blowing through my windows at night. I've always been used to the smell of the peat bog and peat fire, or the moors or the sea."

She felt very sorry for him, although he didn't sound as if he were sorry for himself. He spoke in a matter-of-fact way.

"I expect when you get to boarding school you can open the window," she said.

"Boarding school!" It was as if he had just remembered it. "I've got to have this button business cleared up before I take off for there. I don't want any whisper following me that they'd better keep an eye on the new McGill boy because he's said to be a thief."

"How would a story like that ever get up to St. Ronan's?"

"Ah, who knows how the bad word gets around? In the wind maybe. No, but really, some old biddy woman says to another, 'Did you hear that wild boy Pat McGill stole his grandmother's buttons?' And they talk it over and tell their friends, and it spreads and spreads, the story does, like ripples from a stone you throw in the water. And finally it laps against the shores of St. Ronan's school." He shrugged his shoulders, picked up the glass saucer, emptied the chocolate crumbs into his hand and then dumped them into his mouth. "It's a pig I am," he said, "to be eating up all your candy. You'd better know the worst of me in the beginning. Can you be ready to leave tomorrow morning at half-past seven?"

"How about seven?" she asked. "And I'll bring along some food for lunch."

"Ah that's wonderful. Will you bring along your lion cub?"

She shook her head and answered, "Perhaps I'd better leave him. He might not like the row out in the Clam Shell. I can't see a lion in a rowboat."

"You're right at that." The two laughed. Pat said, "I hope these buttons aren't as imaginary as your lion is."

"Somehow I don't think they are," she said.

"Let's hope not. Okay, I'll be seeing you." He got up, went down the porch steps, turned and called back, "Thanks for the tea and fudge and everything."

As he went toward the hedge, she heard Darlene jumping rope on the terrace and chanting, "Rich boy, poor boy, beggar boy, thief. Patrick, poor boy, beggar boy, thief. Rich boy, poor boy, beggar boy, thief."

Oh how mean, how mean! Janey thought. How absolutely outrageous!

But now, next door, as Pat went through the hedge opening, someone was hushing Darlene and she changed her skipping song to, "Eggs, bacon, coffee, tea; buy your food at the A and P."

Well, I'll fix up a nice big basket of food for us for tomorrow, Janey thought, and got off the hammock. She went into the house and up to her room where she sat down at her desk and wrote letters to her young brother and sister at camp.

Presently, as she was writing, *With love from Janey,* and putting crosses indicating kisses at the bottom of the letter, she heard the whine and buzz of one of the power tools and knew that her father had come home. When she went down the cellar stairs to the workshop, he looked up, smiled at her and shouted, "I'll turn off the racket in a minute."

She nodded and stood watching him, admiring the sure way his hands guided the board so that the dangerous small saw ate right along the line he had drawn. In a moment it had come to the end and he held the two pieces and turned off the power.

"How are things?" he asked, put one of the pieces he had been cutting into the vise of his workbench and took up a plane.

"Things are all right," she answered. "Have you a minute for me to explain something?"

"I've got not only minutes but hours. Sit down and tell me what's on your mind."

She sat perched on a high stool and said, "It's about Pat McGill and some buttons of his grandmother's, at least nobody's quite sure they really exist but the family thinks so and believe Pat stole them."

"Well, that's a dramatic beginning," he said. A long, blond curl of wood fell onto the floor. "Tell me about it." Another curl dropped.

Janey got off the stool and picked them up. She loved the smell of wood and sandpaper, of wax and turpentine and shellac and paints and varnish that always filled the workshop. Back on the stool she fastened the yellow curls in her hair, tying them on by her pony-tail's ribbon.

"Very becoming," her father said. "Now what's all this about Pat?"

She told him the whole thing and now and then he stopped his planing to look up and listen.

"I hope you and the boy can find them," he said, "but I wouldn't set my heart on it. Remember with buried treasure some pirates have usually got there first and left a hole in the sand with a rusted pickax and an old skull and the torn map." He laughed, but very kindly.

"I know, Father, and we won't set out hearts on it. May I help him? Go out to Three Pines Island and everything?"

"Why not? It ought to be fun. I've got to turn on the power saw again and concentrate."

She thanked him, watched him for a moment or two thinking he was wonderful, that there was no father like him. How dreadful it would be if he were like Kit's father, Mr. Barrow! Feeling pleased with her own family and home she went upstairs again to her room, stood before her dressing table and laughed at herself with the long yellow curls of wood shavings.

The last time her grandmother had visited here she had suggested that Janey wear her hair loose, cut to the line of the chin. The ends would probably curl and a bang across the forehead would be becoming. But at that time everybody was wearing pony-tails and Janey hadn't wanted to seem queer and different. Now she thought perhaps her grandmother had been right so she removed the wood curls, loosened the pony-tail, brushed her hair vigorously, took scissors, trimmed it shorter so that it swung to just below the ears and then cut a really becoming bang across the forehead. A page boy's cut! It *was* becoming. It made her look absolutely different, rather dashing and almost glamorous.

As she was standing there she heard an engine start next door. Looking out of the window she saw Pat's small old foreign car back out of the driveway. It was a dark green color and very shabby but she knew Pat loved it. Janey wondered where he was going now and hoped he was not too miserable and would not stay out late, driving around alone.

6

It was a lovely morning, sunny and warm, with a little wind. Pat had put back the top of his convertible, and Janey's hair would have blown all over the place if she hadn't tied a yellow silk handkerchief over it. It was very becoming. She wore faded blue jeans and a cream silk blouse, tailored and well cut, and it suited her. When she had looked in her mirror before starting off, she had been pleased with the girl who smiled back at her—not a bad-looking girl at all. She felt carefree and happy in the low front car seat beside Pat. They had not got off as early as they had meant to because, naturally, Pat had slept late.

To her surprise, he didn't strike right for the shore roads but went into the center of the town and for some minutes had to cruise around looking for a parking meter. Finally he did find one at the edge of the Green and worked his way into the space.

"Do you mind waiting a few minutes," he said. "I want to send some flowers to my grandmother. I think the florist across there is open."

"How is your grandmother?" she asked.

"She's going to have her operation today. My uncle and aunt are going to be at the hospital."

"I do hope everything goes well," she said as he got out.

"I hope so," he answered. As he took coins from his pocket, he asked, "What should I send her? Some orchids?"

That almost took her breath away. She answered, "I wouldn't send orchids, Pat. They're for people going to big parties and dances. If you're sick in bed you want some nice simple flowers, like, like daisies."

"Daisies! They're not nearly good enough."

She watched him putting a dime in the meter, then stride off along the Green toward the florist's ship. He was wearing very old gray flannel slacks with a patch, actually, and the holes showed badly in the sleeves of his thin turtle-neck gray sweater. And he wanted to send his grandmother orchids! He was wonderful, but she couldn't quite make Pat out.

Presently he was back and they were on their way again. Pat drove well, fast but carefully. She knew he would never be one to play the crazy game of chicken and land them in a ditch or wound around a telephone pole. Now they had left the city behind and were on the many-laned highway leading east.

He said, "I went around to the library last night and talked to that librarian who's a friend of yours, Miss Anderson. She looks a bit like a movie star but more human and friendly."

"Oh, she's wonderful. She always helps me. What were you looking up, Pat?"

He said he had wanted to know more about George Washington's inauguration and Miss Anderson had found books for him and places in them. He had sat there reading until the library closed.

"Did you know," he said, "that the poor guy didn't want to be president at all? He said he'd rather be in his grave than be president. And he was all anxious and upset when he left his farm in Mt. Vernon to go to New York. It was a long hard trip then with coaches and horses."

"But they did a lot of traveling by boat too, I think," Janey said.

"They did that. The roads were mostly mud holes. They must have been in bad shape in April when Washington came up to New York."

"What year?" she asked. "I've forgotten."

"Seventeen-eighty-nine. He boarded a 'beautifully decorated barge' at Elizabeth Town point and came up Kill Van Kull, wherever those places are."

"New Jersey, and between New Jersey and Staten Island, I think," Janey said. "Go on, Pat, then what happened?"

"The barge crossed New York harbor and there were people cheering, bands playing, and ships dipping their flags. Oh, it was terrific."

"I would have loved to see it!" Janey's voice showed how much she wished she had been there. "I wonder if Washington was wearing his brown broadcloth suit."

Pat laughed. He said he didn't know when Washington put that on. There was a wonderful description, though, of the day of the ceremonies. New York was full of thousands of visitors. Guns were thundering, bells pealing! The members of Congress and a detachment of soldiers marched, with bands playing, to Washington's home on

Cherry Street. Then they escorted him to a place called Federal Hall. There were ceremonies in the hall and then Washington and some other eminent men went out onto the balcony overlooking Wall Street. With awe in his voice, Pat said, "There were thousands of people watching, all absolutely silent. And then the Secretary of the Senate presented the Bible on a red cushion. The oath of office was administered; Washington kissed the Bible. A man called Chancellor Livingston cried, 'Long live George Washington, President of the United States!' Cheers all but split the clouds, bands played, church bells rang, and cannon boomed from the fort and ships."

"Patrick, it gives me shivers up my spine!" Janey cried. "I do hope we can find his buttons! It would make it all seem so real!"

"You don't want to find them as much as I do. It's no fun, I tell you, to have your relatives think you're a thief and a robber and have them looking at you with sorrow and disapproval in their eyes. And Darlene bounces up and down over her skipping rope, singing, 'Rich boy, poor boy, beggar boy, thief.' The rich boy, of course, is my cousin Ronnie, but she means that all the other terms apply to me."

"She's just a rude little girl," Janey told him. "She's not worth taking seriously."

"I know, and her brother Willie isn't either."

"What does he do to you, except make darts and hit people with them?"

"Oh, he imitates and exaggerates my Irish accent all the time, but what of it. I suppose we've got to let the kids have their fun."

"I don't think much of their idea of fun, hurting people's feelings," Janey was indignant. "My brother and sister don't do it."

"Ah well, they're civilized," Pat said. "Let's forget it. We're going to have a grand day."

He gave the car a little more gas and they went faster, with glittering cars approaching on the lanes beyond the center barrier. There were suburban houses here and there, left and right of the highway, and then fields and trees and a good smell of grass and asters and goldenrod in the wind.

When they reached Green Cove, there were Ben Green and his mother, Mrs. Sally Green, going down to the dock carrying a basket of rags and cleaning powders and such things. Mrs. Sally Green was short and plump with plain gray hair and a nice plain face, pleasant from friendliness and much laughter. Ben Green's foot was still in its cast and bandages.

Pat stopped his car under an apple tree, and Mr. Green shouted out good mornings to Pat and Janey. "If you two are going to Three Pines Island," he said, "could you row Mother out with you?"

"Surely, I'd love to," Pat said.

"Mrs. Barrow telephoned me last night," Mrs. Green said, "I mean your aunt did, Pat. She said your grandmother's having her operation today. I hope everything goes well."

"It should," Ben Green said. "She's a fine strong old lady, I think. Be of good heart, boy. It does no good to worry. Got all your rags, Mother?"

Mrs. Green said she had and explained that Pat's aunt had asked her to go out to the island today and do some cleaning up. "It seems those Goodwards," she said, "*Bad-*

wards I'd call them, pranced themselves off leaving stuff in the icebox and everything at sixes and sevens. At least, they told her they weren't going to be bothered making the house ready for the winter."

Pat said, "I want to pick up some of my clothes and my grandmother asked me to hunt for something for her— and Janey and I hoped we could get in a swim."

"I brought my suit and cap," Janey said.

As they settled themselves in the Clam Shell, Mrs. Sally told them that Janey needn't have bothered to bring her bathing suit. There were plenty of them hanging up in the coat closet under the stairs for guests. Some of these suits were fifty years old and the Barrows' friends wore them sometimes still just to be funny.

Pat was rowing now and was coming to open water. "Did you know my mother when she spent the summers here?" Pat asked.

"Ah, I did, indeed, and a sweet thing, and a pretty one she always was. I'll never forget one terrible night when she and her brother, Mr. Will Barrow, that is, of New Haven, rowed away and lost themselves. Little bits of things they were then. They'd been playing in one of the rowboats at the dock and managed to untie it and off they went in it, nobody seeing them. When it was found they were gone, the family was nearly crazy. You see, there's that dangerous stretch of water called the Styx Channel—never be trying to swim that, Pat McGill, will you?"

He answered, rowing strongly, "My Uncle Will warned me about it when I first went to my grandmother's on the island."

"Yes, well, there's been people lost there. However,

your mother and her brother drifted safe through it and got ashore at Bayberry Bush Island. It used to be bigger in those days before all the hurricanes. It was my husband found them there huddled down in a hollow of sand behind that little hill. It was the middle of the night and they were asleep."

Janey, who was sitting in the bow with the basket of food and a bag holding Pat's swimming equipment, thought how dreadful it would be if her own small brother and sister were lost like that. "Which is Bayberry Bush Island?" she asked and turned to look ahead.

"It's that one in the distance to the right," Mrs. Sally pointed out.

"That sort of sand bar in the water with a little hill and bushes on top?" Janey asked.

"That's it."

"It's about a quarter of a mile from my grandmother's dock," Pat said. "It's not a good place to swim to. As Mrs. Sally says there's a treacherous current sweeping around out there." He pulled on toward Three Pines Island and presently they reached it, landed, and he tied the Clam Shell to the dock.

Once in the house Mrs. Sally went right to work in the kitchen, and Pat and Janey began their search in the living room. It was large and pleasant with windows looking out through trees toward the water. There was a dark, polished floor with old oriental rugs. The chairs and two sofas were deep and comfortable; wicker and brown leather chairs and chintz-covered sofas. The desk and table, the bookcases and tall cabinet for Mrs. Barrow's collection of china were of heavy carved oak. On the walls were oil paintings of cows and landscapes. Also three stuffed deer's heads surveyed the room with yellow glass eyes.

Janey found she couldn't bring herself to do the necessary exploring so she stood by and watched and encouraged Pat. He searched quickly, wasting no time in looking at the various interesting things he came upon. There were cards, road maps, some small games and puzzles in the drawers of the tables; papers, letters, checkbooks, notebooks, writing paper, stamps and pens and pencils in the desk. Below the high glass doors and the shelves of the china cabinet were three long drawers and in these were charts of Long Island Sound. In the dining room there was the silver tea set on the sideboard and linen and silver in the drawers.

Mrs. Sally, working around in the kitchen, called out to Pat to bring some bags down from the attic so that she could pack the silver in them and take it back to her house to keep there until Mrs. Will Barrow could come out for it.

Janey began to feel a little tired of it as the hunt went on upstairs. Here the drawers and closets held only what you would expect: clothes and clothes and clothes, and sheets, blankets, towels and pillow cases. Here in the linen closet was a sweet smell of lavender from little bags of it among the sheets.

"Those buttons might just be hidden in one of these small bag affairs," Pat said, so he and Janey squeezed them all carefully between their fingers but felt only the dried petals and no flat metal disks.

The two went next up steep narrow stairs to the attic, to a smell of old, dry wood, cedar and moth balls. Here, as she stood at the top of the stairs, Janey felt almost as if she had come to an enchanted cave from the Arabian nights. A beam of sunlight streamed in through a half-round, dusty window, but this was not enough to brighten more than the small area around it. The attic stretched away into mysterious darkness where the roof came down to the floor. There seemed to be dozens of trunks and boxes and cedar chests. Pat found a hanging light bulb, turned it on and now they could see more clearly: a suit of armor, a big doll's house, a tall puppet theater with red and white striped curtains.

"That was my mother's," Pat said. "She used to give puppet shows when she was our age."

"Oh, how wonderful!" Janey said. "Oh Pat, do you think she had the characters for her plays?"

"Of course. They're in this box."

She followed him and knelt on the floor as he opened a good-sized carton. Funny little figures stared up at her. They were dusty and somewhat tired-looking hand puppets for all sorts of plays. There was a king and a queen and a princess, a red-riding-hood and savage wolf and grandmother; three little fuzzy gray kittens and a striped mother cat; three little pigs and a mother pig. The red-riding-hood wolf would do for this show too.

"Oh wonderful, wonderful!" Janey said, sitting back on her heels. She slipped the wolf over her hand and made him wave his paws and found that his jaw opened and shut ferociously.

"I could do marvelous performances with these, Pat," Janey said. "I wonder if your grandmother—" But she couldn't say she wondered if Mrs. Barrow, Senior, would ever lend these to her.

"They're mine now," Pat said from beneath the eaves.

"Wouldn't you like to borrow the stage and all those characters?"

"Would I like to? Oh, would I ever like to!"

He laughed a little. Then he opened a trunk lid and, after a moment or two, let it drop down. He came back to Janey carrying a large flat box, sat on the floor and opened it. It was full of the most beautiful lead soldiers she had ever seen, knights riding horseback, jousting, knocking each other off their horses, galloping off triumphantly waving spears and pennants. But Pat was mournfully whistling *The Wearing of the Green*.

Looking at the soldiers, they heard Mrs. Sally Green coming up the attic stairs.

Pat said, in a discouraged tone, "Janey, it would take us three-hundred-and-sixty-five days at least to explore this attic carefully. Needles in haystacks are nothing in comparison with buttons in Mrs. Barrow's attic. If I were not going to school in nine days, if I could stay out here and pitch in and make a thorough job of this I might find them—*if* they're here at all."

She put the princess puppet on her hand and smoothed down the little pink satin dress and straightened the small gilded tin crown.

"If you only had another clue, or a map showing the treasure," she said.

Mrs. Sally had reached the top of the stairs. She was panting a little.

"Oh, I'm sorry we haven't brought the bags down to you," Pat said, and jumped up.

"There's time enough yet," she answered. "I've got lots to do still. Those Goodwards left things in a state, I can tell you." She came further into the attic and sat down on one of the low trunks, folding her hands in her lap. She wore a plain gray dress and a big white apron and the sight of her there was comforting.

She said, "Why don't you two come on down and have your swim? The sun's lovely and it's nice and warm outside. I think you've been fussing around in the dust long enough, don't you really?"

"We ought to find those things for my grandmother if we can," Pat answered, doubtfully.

Janey knew he had had just about all of this searching he could stand at present, but he was the sort who wouldn't give up easily.

Mrs. Sally said, "You'd better plan to move in here and spend five years at it then, Pat. I wouldn't undertake it for less."

He gave a small sigh and said, "I've just thought of something. We'll have to take all the books in the house out of their shelves and look behind them."

"Oh heavens!" Janey exclaimed and pulled the princess puppet off her hand. She too was feeling that she had had about all of the dusty attic that she could endure, fascinating though it was.

Mrs. Sally said, "Now look, Pat McGill. I've known your mother and all your uncles and I loved her—your mother. And I've known and worked for and liked your grandmother for fifty years and more. I heard that broadcast on the television about collections, and that made me remember, and a lot of other people remembered around here too, I'm afraid, that she was supposed to have some of George Washington's buttons hidden here. It's them you're trying to find, isn't it?"

"Yes, it is," Pat admitted. "And I've got to find them

and take them to my uncle Will because he and Aunt Cindy, and Ronnie and Kit and Willie and Darlene all think I've stolen them."

"Poppycock! Poppycock!" Mrs. Sally answered, indignantly. "I never heard anything so silly in my life. They're right here in this house somewheres. As I was cleaning out the icebox downstairs, it suddenly came to me."

"What came to you," Pat and Janey demanded, at once, loudly.

"Something your grandma, Pat, said to me years ago—thirty—forty years ago, maybe more. She said, 'You know those boys of mine have been reading ghost stories and they're wild to find some silver buttons. You can only kill a ghost by shooting him with a silver button. I'm afraid they'll get hold of those Washington ones and lose them, unless I hide them in a good safe place. I'll follow the example of Mrs. Lecks and Mrs. Aleshine, and the rent money.'"

"Mrs. Lex and Mrs. Aleshine?" Janey repeated.

"Who were they?" Pat asked. "Who in thunder were Mrs. Lex and Mrs. Aleshine?"

"That I don't know," Mrs. Sally answered. "Probably some friends of hers. I used to meet some of her friends, but of course not all of them."

"It's a real clue!" Janey cried. "It's the first clue! No, the second. The first clue was the books."

"I think you're right!" Pat agreed. "Thanks, Mrs. Green. Thanks a lot. Now we've got something to go on. All we have to do is to find Mrs. Lex and Mrs. Aleshine."

"How will we go about it?" Janey asked, feeling excited.

"We'll look up all the Lexes and Aleshines in the New

Haven telephone book. But, oh my gosh, what if they were New York friends, or lived somewhere else? What if we had to look up Lexes and Aleshines all over the country?"

Janey said, "Well, it doesn't do to think of that. What if men climbing Everest thought of all the awful things that *might* happen to them?"

"I guess they do," he replied. "I guess they have to. You've got to be prepared."

"Well, it's lucky we don't have to be equipped with tents and furs and climbing shoes and oxygen tanks and pemmican and everything else under the sun for those expeditions. All we need are some telephone books. Come on down, Pat. I'm absolutely dying for a swim."

Entirely forgetting Mrs. Sally Green's suitcase for the silver, they went pounding down the stairs.

Soon they were swimming off the dock in the island's little harbor. For a time Mrs. Sally Green sat on the dock, knitting, her back against a high pile. The knitting needles glinted in the sun.

Janey wore a tight peppermint-candy striped swimming suit with a pink cap, extremely becoming. But Pat, she thought, was like a figure from outer space in his black skin-diver's suit reaching to wrists and ankles, and with his fins and green mask and snorkle. He stayed under water so long that it worried her, but both she and Mrs. Sally, before they went back up to the house, were soon convinced that he was an exceptionally able and experienced swimmer. Janey herself was good at it, and a beautiful diver. She raced Pat and was gratified that he beat her by only about ten yards.

"You know, you're not half bad," he told her as they

climbed up onto the dock. "You ought to train for the real thing—Scuba. Oh gosh, how I wish I had an aqua-lung! Two hundred dollars! I might as well want to buy a ninety-foot yacht!" He was taking off his mask and the fins on his feet.

"You're hungry," Janey said, hopping around on one foot to drain water from her ear. "Whenever my father's or Jimmie or May's voices sound sunk and discouraged like that I rush and get them something to eat."

"Here comes Mrs. Green now with the lunch basket," he said and ran up the steep path to help her.

They sat in the lovely sun on the dock and ate ham sandwiches and egg and celery sandwiches and drank ginger ale and then ate sweet, juice-dripping pears and delicious chocolate cupcakes with white icing. The air was warm and filled with the good smell of pines and water. Sunlight shivered on high pine needles, and sunlight was sprinkled on the water. Mrs. Green, knitting away, told them about a lame tame crow she used to have who liked to swing by its beak from the corners of sheets hung out to dry, and often would take off the heads of flowers in a neighbor's garden. And Pat, lying on his back in the sun, told of a little pig he used to have in Ireland and how it would come in the house sometimes, and how it liked tea and would look up and grunt disapprovingly if there wasn't enough milk and sugar with it.

But finally the wind got cooler, and Mrs. Sally Green said she didn't want them catching cold and they'd better pack up and be off.

"I'm awfully obliged to you for that clue about those two friends of my grandmother's," Pat said, getting up and holding out his hand to Janey to pull her to her feet.

"We'll go right back and try to locate them through the telephone book."

"Don't let yourself think it's going to be too hard," Janey told him. "And remember, this isn't the sort of exploration where we'll be falling down crevasses. Come on, we'll have to hurry and dress."

7

It was late in the morning of the next day before Pat and Janey could take up their search again. Pat had to go downtown with his aunt to buy clothes for school and he came over to the Murrays' in a depressed state. She had noticed before that buying clothes always cast boys and men into irritation or gloom whereas it swung girls up into heights of happiness. Pat was whistling *The Wearing of the Green* again, like a funeral march, like a dirge, and that always meant he was at a low point.

She had been letting down the hem in one of her blue school uniforms when he came up the steps. She opened the screen door for him and asked how his grandmother was and he said that the hospital reported her condition "satisfactory." Then Janey asked him if he had got the clothes and he said they had, such as they were; the tweeds over here couldn't compare with those in Ireland and England and they cost the earth. He only hoped his guardian would send a check on for them before all this morning's shopping brought the Barrows to the verge of bankruptcy.

"I don't believe they'll have to go around begging yet," she said. "Come on, Pat, let's look up Aleshines and Lexes."

They went into the pantry and Pat put the telephone book on the sink and flapped pages. He read aloud, "'Alesandrine, Alesandrini, Alesandro, Aleschin, Aleshin, Aleshine Robert B, Aleshine Mary, Aleshine C. D., Aleshine John, Aleshine, Mrs. L. P.' Now, shall we begin with Aleshine, Robert B?"

"I would," she answered. "Dial that number and ask for Mrs. Aleshine. If she is a friend of your grandmother's, she'll have an old voice."

"Yes, I suppose so."

"What will you say?" Janey asked. She began to feel a little doubtful about this.

"I'll just ask her if she knows my grandmother and if she'd mind telling me what she did with her rent money around forty years ago." He was dialing numbers.

"Oh heavens!" Janey said, quickly. "You can't put it like that. She'll think you're crazy."

"Why should she? It's just a straightforward question."

Janey had an impulse to grab the telephone away from him. But he had the number and was already speaking. He was saying, "Oh good morning, is this Mrs. Aleshine? This is Patrick McGill. I'm afraid you don't know me but —no, I'm not trying to sell magazines—no, Mrs. Aleshine, I'm not trying to sell anything. I just want to ask a question. No it's not for a poll—it's not. Hello, hello—" He looked at Janey. "What do you know?" he said. "The woman hung up on me. We'll try Aleshine, Mary, next."

"Look, Pat," Janey said, "I think you ought to approach this very, very tactfully, sort of lead them into it. You know, it's really an awfully odd thing to ask anyone."

"Still I've got to ask it if I'm to have any reputation left me. I've got to re-establish my good name before I go off to school." He was dialing SP 5-2295. "Oh, good afternoon," he said. "Might I speak with Miss Mary Aleshine? Oh, you say she's gone to California. Would you happen to know if she was a friend of Mrs. Barrow?"

Janey heard a cross voice crackling out an answer that did not seem to be encouraging.

"Could you tell me if Miss Mary Aleshine is an elderly lady? It's quite important that I find out. Well, I suppose you might say I am a detective of sorts. No, it's not really a police matter as yet. No, I can't explain it. I assure you," and this he said stiffly and politely, "I am not playing any sort of a trick on anyone." After a moment he looked at Janey and said, "She hung up too."

Mrs. C. D. Aleshine was out at a luncheon and there was no Mrs. John Aleshine. He dialed the proper numbers and presently got Aleshine, Mrs. L. P. Again he said good morning and gave his name politely, but Janey wished that his voice sounded a little less Irish, although it was actually more Oxford than Irish, that is, when he was being formal as now.

Janey began to feel more and more tense as she listened, because this conversation was not going well.

He was saying, "Mrs. Aleshine, I'm trying to find an old friend of my grandmother's, Mrs. Clarence Barrow. You see, she has lost some buttons, very valuable buttons, and I'm trying to find them for her. And it seems that forty or fifty years ago she hid them away somewhere in the same sort of place where a Mrs. Aleshine put her rent money. Could you—"

"Oh heavens, oh heavens!" Janey exclaimed in a low voice and hugged her arms around herself to keep from bursting out into nervous laughter. It sounded so ridiculous, so absolutely crazy.

"No, please, just a minute, Mrs. Aleshine," Pat was saying, "please, I don't mean to be at all rude. But couldn't you tell me where you used to put your rent money? I'm sorry. No, I'm very sorry. Good-by then."

"She was in a rage," he said, seeming surprised. "She was in an utter fury and threatened to call the police. What's the matter with you, now?"

She gasped, "But, Pat, it's frightfully funny. Can't you see how you'd feel if the telephone rang and you rushed to it and a boy's voice asked if you were a friend of his grandmother and said she'd lost some buttons, and he was trying to find them for her and did you mind telling what you'd done with the rent money fifty years ago?" She went into a gale of laughter and he, after a moment or two, grinned and laughed too.

They stood in the pantry, leaning against the sink, laughing until they were weak. The black cat meowed in the kitchen and Janey welcomed it into the pantry and picked it up and it began to purr.

"Come on, let's have some lunch," she suggested. "You don't have to go back to the Barrows for it, do you?"

"They don't have what I call lunch there," he told her. "It's always peanut butter and some sort of jelly sandwiches and I hate peanut butter."

"How about bacon and eggs and tomato juice and some ice-cold rice pudding with lots of raisins in it and some cream on top."

"Keen!" he told her. "Absolutely keen."

They went into the kitchen and she got eggs from the refrigerator while he sat at the table and stroked the cat.

"Let's drive around right after lunch to see the Lexes," Janey said. "I think perhaps we'd make a better impression if we asked those questions face to face."

"Maybe you'll get along with them better than I have," he answered. "I seem to make them mad with the first word I say."

She, tactfully, changed the subject and asked about skin-diving and his study of jellyfish in Florida. So, as they ate lunch, he became much more cheerful and by the time they were finished and had washed the dishes they were ready to hunt up Lexes and go out to interview them.

After looking in the telephone book and finding Lewey, Lewy, Lewyckyl, Lewyn and Lewyt there were eight Lexes, sprinkled all over the city of New Haven.

"It doesn't do any good to put it off," Pat said. "Come on, let's go."

It was a hot afternoon, sticky and humid. People on the streets seemed tired and unattractive. There was a lot of traffic and drivers were cross. Several of them shouted out at Pat, quite unnecessarily, "Hi dope, where do you think you're going?" and three or four times they tooted their horns at him angrily. He drove to the addresses of two Lexes who lived in apartment houses. He and Janey walked up flights of stairs amid smells of cooking, only to find that no one answered the doorbells and, disappointed, they went down. Again, at a small pink frame house on a side street only a yapping dog inside paid any attention to the bell. One Lex lived near the harbor and they drove there to an old, three-story brick house. A young woman with her hair in curlers stuck her head out of a window and shouted down that yes, she was Mrs. Lex and she didn't know any Mrs. Barrow and what was it all about anyway. Next, across the park and in a little shopping section, there was a small stationery and confectionery store with *A.Lex* above the door on an awning. Inside a middle-aged Italian woman stood behind the counter. She could scarcely speak a word of English.

"I don't think she would have been a friend of your grandmother's," Janey said in a low tone.

Pat bought ten cents worth of gum drops, thanked the woman and went on out.

The next place they went to was a small ranch-type house in a new development. Here the door was opened quickly, but only opened a crack. They could see only part of a woman and got an impression of black hair, suspicion, a frilly pink flowered apron, and an angry voice.

"Yes, I'm Mrs. Lex," the woman answered. "What is it? I don't want to take any chances or buy any girl scout cookies."

"It's not that at all, Mrs. Lex," Pat said. "We're not selling anything."

"What is it then? I've a cake in the oven."

Janey thought it remarkable that this person ever did anything as pleasant as baking cake.

"You explain. You tell her," Pat said.

Janey had thought she could do it so much better than he. She had thought it would be easy, but it wasn't. Her voice seemed caught in her throat. She said, "You see, the point is that we're trying to locate a Mrs. Lex who was a friend of Pat's—this is Pat—a friend of Pat's grandmother, Mrs. Barrow, Mrs. Clarence Barrow."

"Barrow?" the woman opened the door a bit wider. From inside an old, petulant voice called, "Who is it, Manty?"

"Some kids. I can't make out what they want. What is it now?" she said to them. "Barrow? There was a Clarence Darrow in the papers a long time ago, something about monkeys and a law suit."

"This isn't Darrow, it's *Barrow*," Pat explained.

"It's nothing to do with monkeys. It's buttons," Janey said, and wished she hadn't.

"Buttons!" The door closed a bit more.

"Yes, my grandmother lost her buttons; I mean, she mislaid some very valuable buttons and we're trying to find—"

"I don't know a thing about any buttons I always use zippers." The woman's voice rose. "If you're accusing me of taking any buttons off a woman named Barrow I've never seen or heard of her, to my knowledge!"

"But would perhaps your mother-in-law have known about them?" Janey felt desperate, and there *was* an old woman somewhere in the house here. She felt that they were almost on the track of something important, and she noticed that Pat had slipped the toe of his sneaker inside the door.

"I haven't got any mother-in-law," the woman said, "and I haven't got any more time to waste on you two. Good-by—"

"Just a minute, just one minute, please!" Janey implored. "Just tell us what you used to do with your rent money—or what your husband's mother used to do with her rent money."

"You two are crazy!" the woman cried. "Buttons and

rent money! I pay my rent to the landlord, who else. Get away with you. If it's your idea of a joke, it's not mine!" She tried to slam the door but Pat's toe was in it and got squeezed.

He removed his foot quickly and he and Janey looked at each other. He said, "Phew! Nice character, isn't it!" and went limping after Janey down the steps and offered her the little bag of gum drops, then took one himself.

Mrs. Lex's lawn was smooth and green. Three ornamental spotted deer made of plaster or some substance like it lay on the grass. It was a great relief to leave that place and get into Pat's car.

"What next?" he asked, stepping on the starter. For a moment he sat frowning and then he began to whistle *The Wearing of the Green* again.

Janey said, "Let's stop at a drugstore and get a strawberry float and then decide what we ought to do. We'll feel better after we've had something to eat."

He grinned at her, said, "Okay," and drove on away from that horrid experience. But they hadn't gone more than half a mile when Pat began to laugh. "I don't blame her so much," he said. "She must have thought we were absolutely nuts!"

It was just as they were going into the largest drugstore in New Haven, the one on the busiest corner, when they met Miss Anderson, the librarian, going in as well. She wore a thin, striped cotton suit, tan and white, crisp and cool looking, and her hair was dark and perfectly waved. Besides all this, she looked like a friend, a person who could appreciate why one did odd things, a person who would surely understand and not disapprove.

She said, "Hello, you two. Could I interest you in some ice cream or something cooling?"

They answered that they were just going to get something, they were rather hot but she mustn't bother.

"No bother at all," she told them. "Come on now. Let me. I'd like to. Give your order."

She ordered a lemon sherbert but urged them to have something more filling, something perhaps with nuts and whipped cream on top—the works, why not. So the three stood at the cool counter and let delicious sweet cold mouthfuls slip down their hot throats and they began to feel better.

After a minute or two Miss Anderson asked in a casual way, "How is the research getting on?"

"Research?" Janey asked.

"George Washington, buttons and so on. Or perhaps it's more search than research now. Is it?"

"It is," Janey admitted, and she turned to Pat and said, "Oh Pat, let's tell her something about it. I think perhaps she could help us."

"Yes, let's see if I can't help you," Miss Anderson said. "What's the problem?"

"The point is," Janey said, and wondered if Miss Anderson would think her as crazy as the other woman had, "the point is that we want to find out where Mrs. Lex and Mrs. Aleshine hid their rent money. But we've been in touch with all the Lexes and Aleshines in New Haven and they shut the doors in our faces when we ask."

It seemed to Janey that Miss Anderson would have liked to laugh, but she didn't.

"There were eight L-E-X's in the telephone book," Pat

said. He turned his spoon upside down and licked the bowl of it.

"I imagine it's usually spelled L-E-C-K-S," Miss Anderson told them. "Come along to the library and I think I can find something that will help you solve that problem. I've been wanting to see you about it anyway." She paid at the cashier's booth. It was not an inexpensive treat and Pat and Janey thanked her with much appreciation. They felt a great deal better now, and cooler, and more hopeful.

Soon they were in the reading room of the library, sitting at a heavy, long oak table where there were no other readers. They waited for a few minutes. Janey whispered to Pat and asked him how his foot felt, the one the woman had squashed in the door.

"It wasn't quite entirely squashed," he answered. "I don't think any bones are broken." Then he and Janey stood up as Miss Anderson came back with a pale grayish green book.

She put it on the table and said, "Sit down. I have something to tell you that I think you should know about this project of yours."

Janey's heart almost sank. It seemed to her that Miss Anderson's voice sounded as if she had some bad news to tell. The three sat down and Miss Anderson said, "I've been doing a bit of detective work for you two, telephoning here and there."

"That's very kind of you," Pat said.

"I don't know whether or not you'll be pleased about this, but George Washington's brown broadcloth inaugural coat is in a museum in Morristown, New Jersey."

"Now?" Pat and Janey exclaimed together, and Janey wondered if Pat felt as shocked as she did.

"I'm afraid so, and it has buttons on it, but they're covered with brown cloth."

Pat sat staring at her.

Janey said, wretchedly, "Then all that about the big gilt buttons was a myth, after all."

"We mustn't jump to conclusions," Miss Anderson said. "There may have been other original ones which were cut off and handed around as souvenirs and these cloth-covered ones might have been put on later. Or one or two of the gilt ones may simply have been lost, and Mrs. Washington may have had these put on, as a whole new set."

"Oh yes, of course!" Janey agreed. "Don't look so sad about it, Pat. Of course that's probably what happened. I'm sure Mrs. Washington wouldn't have been so foolish as to waste her time covering beautiful gilt buttons engraved with the United States seal, with an eagle and scroll and everything, with brown cloth. It wouldn't make sense, and I'm sure Martha Washington was a sensible woman, don't you think so, Miss Anderson?"

"I do." Miss Anderson laughed a little, quietly, in order not to disturb other readers in the big room. "Look here," she said, "I talked to a friend of mine in Hartford who has a large button collection and she thinks that the original gilt ones do exist. Several people claim they have some, but she says they may be mistaken. This friend of mine thinks it's worthwhile for you to keep on hunting."

"That's good news then," Pat said. "We'll keep on with it, shall we, Janey?"

"I couldn't bear to give up now," she answered.

"Good then," Miss Anderson said. "I hoped you'd feel like that. Now this book I've brought you is *The Casting*

Away of Mrs. Lecks and Mrs. Aleshine by Stockton and I think you'll find something to help you in here." She smiled at them, got up and went back to the information desk.

Pat opened the book and he and Janey looked at it together. It seemed to be a story about a man and two women, a Mrs. Lecks and Mrs. Aleshine, who were on a steamer that was wrecked in the Pacific. They rowed away in a small, leaky boat and finally got to an island, deserted, but with a large, comfortable European house on it. The book had amusing pictures. Pat and Janey skimmed over the pages.

"Look, look," Janey said. "Now this Mrs. Lecks is beginning to worry about paying her board—her rent, that is."

"We're getting closer," Pat said. "We're getting there."

"Here it is!" Janey's voice was almost too loud for a library.

"Shhhh," Pat warned her. "Where is it?"

Her finger pointed to a line on page sixty-nine and she read, " 'The board money's in the ginger jar and our consciences is free.' "

The two looked at each other. Janey closed the book. The cover design was composed of lines that were supposed to represent waves, also two small fish, the title in gold and—a fat jar. Mrs. Barrow had three or four like it in her china cabinet in the living room of Three Pines Island.

"Let's go," Pat said and stood up. "Let's drive right out to Green Cove and row out to the island and come back with the buttons in my pocket."

"Tomorrow," she said. "Not tonight. Mrs. Kenney is at

a birthday party for one of her nephews and I must rush home to get my father his supper."

He said, "Oh, all right then. I suppose I'd better make myself a little agreeable to my relatives and I want to find out about my grandmother. Don't say a word about this ginger jar affair, Janey. This is some development, isn't it! It really is good."

They took the book back to the information desk and thanked Miss Anderson, feeling seventy-five per cent happier than fifteen minutes before.

"Find what you wanted?" she asked.

"We did," Janey answered. "It's wonderful."

"If I can help you again, don't hesitate to come in." She added in a voice so low that nobody else could hear her, "Perhaps you'll let me be a silent partner."

"We'd absolutely adore to have you," Janey replied.

Thanking her again, they went out through the wide doors and down the marble steps to the sidewalk. "She's wonderful, isn't she," Janey said.

"She surely is," he replied. They were walking along opposite the Green toward the meter where he had parked his car. "But she makes me feel a little as if I were going about like Sherlock Holmes with a peaked hat and a plaid coat with a cape, and a pipe in my mouth. Do I look like that?"

"Exactly," she answered. "At least, maybe you do give sort of a Sherlock Holmes-like impression. Your face is a bit like his, only younger. Hurry up; we'd better run or our hour will be over and you'll have a ticket."

But when they reached the parking meter they had exactly three minutes to spare.

8

Early the next afternoon Mr. Green himself took Pat and Janey out to Three Pines Island in his outboard motorboat. He was anxious to know about Pat's grandmother and was relieved to hear that she was doing well. He had to see about Mrs. Barrow's generating system, draining it and so on for the winter. His foot was still in its cast and it wasn't easy for him to walk. When they reached the island he limped off slowly, beyond the boathouse to the little building where the generator was kept. He had given Patrick the key to the big house. It was always kept locked during the months when no one was living on the island. The shutters would be closed over the windows later in the fall.

Now when Janey went into the front hall with Pat she felt the loneliness contained in the rooms of houses shut up and left to themselves, their families scattered. There was a chilly feeling in the air, and a smell of sweetish old wood, of rugs and of brass and furniture polish. A clock on the living-room mantle seemed to tick more loudly than clocks ever do, as if it were calling, "Come, look at me, look at me, see if I am all right, if I can still remember how to tell the time."

She and Pat went into the big room and stood side by side looking at Mrs. Barrow's tall china cabinet. The light fell on the glass doors so that they mirrored Pat and Janey, a boy and a girl in blue jeans and sports shirts, his green and hers blue, his hair red and crew-cut and hers soft, dark and becomingly straight except where it curled naturally at its ends, an inch or so above her shoulders. Then, through the reflection of Pat and herself, Janey saw Mrs. Barrow's collection of jars. There were three fat blue and white ones on the next to the top shelf.

"Ginger jars!" she exclaimed.

"That's right," he agreed, brought up a strong straight chair and opened the cabinet doors. They were not locked; in fact, a folded card had been pushed under one of them to keep it closed. As the door swung open, he said to Janey, "You feel in the jars, won't you? My hand is so big, it'd never go in the openings. Besides which, I'm such a clumsy oaf I'd probably bring the whole production down on my head."

She took off her sneakers, said he wasn't at all a clumsy oaf and climbed up on the chair. She took one of the jars from the shelf, looked into its dark opening, saw nothing, felt around inside and found nothing, except some natural bumps and roughnesses of the inner surface. "Not in this one," she said and, disappointed, put it back and took down another.

Her fingers, moving around inside this one, encountered something. "Oh!" she exclaimed. "Oh, Patrick!"

Excitement came into his face. "Are they there?" he asked.

She felt little oval articles, sticky ones. She brought one out and it was a candy Easter egg, blue and very dusty. There were others of all colors, faded, and she held these in the palm of her hand so that Pat could see them.

He touched one and said, soberly, "I suppose one Easter the family must have come out here and had an egg hunt."

Janey knew he was thinking that perhaps his mother, when she was a little girl, had been one of the children searching around this room for candy eggs. And here he was engaged upon another hunt, and one more serious and important for his whole future. As she dropped the eggs back and returned the jar to its shelf, she was realizing what it might mean for a boy to have the reputation of being a thief, to have other boys at boarding school saying, "Don't leave any cash around if Pat McGill is your roommate!" What a bad thing it would be to have all the Barrow uncles and aunts and cousins telling each other that everybody was sure he found the Washington buttons and sold them to buy his aqua-lung.

"Oh Pat!" she said, "I do hope they're in one of these two."

But they weren't. There were four curtain hooks in one and a dried-up cricket in the other. She squealed when she tipped that out onto her hand.

"Shall we hunt through all the other jars and vases?" she suggested, looking down at Pat.

"I don't think there's any use. These definitely are like Mrs. Lecks' and Mrs. Aleshine's ginger jar. So that's that." He began to whistle *The Wearing of the Green.*

"Let's go out and sit on the dock in the sun," she suggested, and wished she had brought along something to eat.

They sat on the end of the dock with their legs dangling and soon the warmth and sunlight cheered Pat a little. They heard Mr. Green hammering away at something in the distance, and they heard a train whistle faintly on the mainland. Here, above them, sea gulls came to see if they had any food to offer and the birds swooped and circled and called to each other. Water lapped with a pleasant sound around the piles of the dock.

Pat was looking over toward Bayberry Bush Island. "That's very treacherous water around there," he said. "There are hidden rocks, submerged, about fifty feet nearer here and the current swirls in and out with a lot of force. My grandmother told me once it was called the Styx current."

"Sticks current?" Janey asked, puzzled.

"S-t-y-x" he spelled it. "We're always getting our x's and c-k-s's mixed."

"So we are. You mean this was named after that river in Greek mythology?"

"That's right—where the old boy with a long white beard ferried souls over from the land of the living to the land of the shades."

"Gracious," she said. "Let's never swim over there."

"We'd better not. I did once and found it really rough. I was glad enough to get out of it."

She thought it must have been rather a bad experience. Pat was always given to understatement.

"I wish I'd brought my wet-suit—my skin-diver's suit— and fins and so on," he said, and he began to pick splinters from a crack in the dock and flipped them off into the water.

Janey felt relaxed and sleepy, but there was something she had been wondering about. She said, "Something I don't understand. Why do your uncle and aunt and your cousins feel so sure you found and took those buttons?"

"Because of what the Goodwards said," he answered, gloomily. "They simply lied about it. As a matter of fact, I think before I rowed them ashore that noon when they were leaving, that she went through my pockets and found an old button in them."

Janey felt a cold sensation in her throat. "Pat!" she said, "What do you mean?" It would be ghastly if he were going to say he had taken them.

"Now don't you begin to doubt me," he told her, quickly. "I've had an old British uniform button lucky piece ever since I was six years old. One of my ancestors was an officer in the British Army in India. He was a very brave guy and got the V.C., a medal of honor."

"I know," she replied. "After all, I do read a book now and then, Patrick McGill."

"Do you now? I thought nobody learned to read in this country until second-year high, as you all call it."

She saw that he was teasing her and told him that she'd like to push him into the water.

He laughed and lay down on his back on the dock.

"What about the brass button lucky piece?" she asked.

"Well, this ancestor of mine died, was shot in an engagement beyond the Indian border, and somehow my father's mother was sent some of his things. There were buttons among them, and my father gave me one and I've carried it around in my pockets ever since. But it disappeared that last day here, and I swear I think Mrs. Goodward took it and showed it to my Uncle Will, and everybody thought it was one of the valuable ones."

"You know they just might," Janey admitted. "People don't know much on this subject."

"True enough."

She said, "But why does Mrs. Goodward seem to dislike you so, Pat?"

"Oh, because I'm a foreigner, and then there was another reason." He went on to explain that the Goodwards had a fifteen-year-old grandson who had wanted a job this summer for six weeks or so, and they had thought it would be a fine thing if Mrs. Barrow, Senior, would hire him as an odd-job boy on the island. They said he could sail with Pat and be a companion to him. "But I told my grandmother it wasn't in the least necessary for her to pay out good money for a companion for me. I was quite used to being on my own. I told her, and I suppose it wasn't very tactful, that I wasn't keen about the guy anyway. I met him once over at the Greens' and I thought he seemed a shifty character. I'm afraid Mrs. Goodward heard me saying that. She used to lurk around outside of doors and listen. So naturally she took an even worse prejudice against me and couldn't say enough bad things about me. Perfectly natural."

Janey said, indignantly, "But she's breaking one of the ten commandments. She's been bearing false witness against her neighbor."

He put his arm across his eyes to keep the sun out of them and said, sleepily, "Oh well, I suppose the poor deluded female honestly thinks I stole them. Here I'm thinking she took my lucky piece. I wish I knew what's become of it. I wish I knew—" He sat up suddenly. "Janey!" he exclaimed. "What a dumb cluck I've been. Here the answer's been staring me in the face. You know that night when the two guys were in the living room and I was peering at them from the stairs? Well, one was scrabbling around on the floor among those broken pieces of blue and white china. That must have been another ginger jar."

"Probably it was. It must have been!"

"And that guy in the white hat, the frightened one, grabbed up a white rag sort of an affair and stuck it in his pocket. I thought he'd dropped *his* handkerchief, but perhaps it was one of my grandmother's and the buttons were wrapped up in it. How about it? How about that, Janey?"

The two sat staring at each other in increasing excitement.

"But of course!" she cried. "They were in that white handkerchief or napkin or whatever it was and he stuffed them into his pocket—"

"For a trophy. The other guy kept telling him he had to bring back a trophy to convince the initiation board."

"Glory, what a trophy he did pick!" she said. "Pat, now the only thing we have to do is to find that boy."

"Yes, that's all," he agreed. "Just find that one boy out of all the millions in the U.S.A. Nothing to it. Absolutely nothing in the world to it. We might advertise." His tone was ironical. "We'll put an advertisement in the *New Haven Register,* 'Will the boy in the white sailor's hat, the frightened one who entered Mrs. Barrow's house on Three Pines Island recently and took some valuable George Washington buttons out of her ginger jar, please communicate with Patrick McGill and Janey Murray of Maple Street, New Haven, and find himself in jail.' "

Janey laughed at him. She said that would scarcely persuade anybody to come forward, would it?

"This is worse than thinking we had to search through my grandmother's attic," he said.

"And worse than getting in touch with all those angry Mrs. Lexes and Mrs. Aleshines."

They laughed again. The farther away they got from that experience the funnier it seemed.

"Should we go to the police?" she suggested. "The police are wonderful about finding missing persons."

"Or a private eye?" he asked. "I wish I had money enough for a private eye."

They were sitting there, thinking, when they heard limping footsteps behind them and there was Mr. Green coming down onto the dock. He was holding a white sailor's cap. "Is this yours, Pat?" he asked. "I found it wedged between two rocks up near the path."

"What do you know?" Pat said quietly in awe and put out his hand for it. "What do you know?" and turned it over and over, looking at it.

"Is it the frightened boy's hat?" Janey asked, almost whispering.

"It must be. I think it is." He looked up at Mr. Green and said, "Thanks awfully. I think this may be a real clue. I think it belongs to one of the boys who were in the house that night. I told you about them."

Mr. Green nodded. "It might be," he agreed.

Janey and Pat got up and the three stood looking at the cap. It was one of these autographed affairs. Jive phrases and girls' names, stick men and hearts, had been inked on it, but it had rained and the ink had run and it was almost impossible to make out words.

Janey said, "Here seem to be some bars of music and a treble clef and some notes."

The others agreed that she was right. "The guy must like music," Pat said. "And look, here's a name: Jeannie Lee Ames."

"And here's another." Janey was turning the cap carefully in her hands. "Here's something that seems to be Kitten, Kitten something, but it's all blurred."

"Kitten Grymes, maybe," Mr. Green said. "You know this is just like Sherlock Holmes. There are some Ameses live on Davenport Street in Branford and two or three Grymes near here, up away from the water, on Drew Street, and two families of them on Apple Tree Lane. Brothers built next door to each other. You know, I shouldn't be surprised if those boys go to our high school. Seems to me I heard one of the clubs there was having an initiation this week."

"Those girls, Jeannie Lee Ames and Kitten Grymes might know who this hat belongs to," Janey cried. "Shall we go and hunt them up now, or what? What do you think, Mr. Green?"

He scratched his head and said, "Unless you drive on home now, it's going to be awfully late when you two get back to New Haven."

"And Mrs. Kenney's out and I have to make some sort of a decent supper for father again," Janey said. "I think we'd better go home now, Pat, and, if you can, drive out again tomorrow afternoon."

They were certainly in a far happier mood when Mr. Green took them ashore in his boat and they drove home in Pat's ramshackle but wonderful little car.

9

Early the next morning when Janey was brushing her hair, she looked out of the window and, beyond the privet hedge, saw Pat washing his car in the Barrows' driveway. Then Darlene came out across the terrace and began to chant, "Rich boy, poor boy, beggar boy, thief," again and again. Next Willie came out, a small boy who was too fat, wearing tan shorts and a striped jersey.

"Ah sure, Pat, begorrah," he said in a loud, exaggerated Irish accent, "begorrah now, don't ye keep pigs in yer parlor in Ireland? And don't ye cook over an open fire in the one room? Sure ye do now. Sure!"

Standing by the window, Janey saw Pat throw a soaking wet sponge. It hit Willie just below the chin and the child roared out, "Marmee, Marmee, Daddy, Pat threw a sponge at me!" He ran up onto the terrace, shouting, "A soaking wet sponge all dirty water."

Darlene joined in, crying out, "A horrible wet sponge, right in poor Willie's face. His clothes are *ruined!*" The two ran into the house, slamming the long screen door.

Janey ran downstairs quickly, out across the porch and grass and stood in the opening of the hedge. Howls and weeping came from the Barrows' house. Pat stood polishing the hood of his car, looking unhappy.

Janey called, "Pat, could you come over a minute?"

He looked up, nodded and took long strides to the hedge. The two went over to the Murray house and stood below the porch. He said, "Now the skies will fall on me surely."

"Why should they?" she asked, indignantly. "I wonder you didn't turn the hose on those children. They're absolutely maddening."

"Ah well, they're young, they're uncivilized," he answered. "I shouldn't ever be losing my temper at them." Then, changing the subject, he said, "Can you drive out to Green Cove again with me this afternoon so we can hunt up Jeannie Lee Ames and Kitten Grymes?"

She answered that she thought she could come in the afternoon. She had to buy some school clothes for herself and for Jimmie and May this morning. "And anyway," she said, "probably Jeannie Lee and Kitten Grymes are in school until three o'clock. The public schools began last week, you know."

"I know. I have only a week before I have to be off to Saint Ronan's, seven more days to show my relatives I'm not a thief and a robber and a vandal. What school do you go to, Janey?"

"Saint Brigit's, up on the top of the hill."

"Ah, Saint Brigit," he said and smiled. "She was one of my favorite saints. How many more days before you have to go back?" he asked.

"It opens the day after your school does."

"Ah good. Seven days. Can we do it in seven days, do you think?"

She smiled and said, "Doesn't the Bible say the world was made in seven days? That was a much bigger project, Patrick."

"Well, it was at that," he agreed, also smiling, "and whether it was meant symbolically or not we ought to be able to do a little thing like finding six buttons."

"Who ever said there were six?" she asked. "There may have been more, don't you suppose?"

"There may have been ten or twelve, or three or two maybe." He stood still a moment, listening. No more howls came from the Barrows' house. Pat said, in relief, "It looks as if my uncle and aunt aren't going to make a big deal out of the sponge incident, and I'm glad too. Peaceful co-existence, that's what I strive for, like the nations."

She thought, He's wonderful! He's one of the nicest people I've ever known in my life.

"This afternoon then for Green Cove," he said. "I'll be seeing you."

As they drove out from the city that afternoon the sky became overcast and looked as if there would be rain before night. Both Pat and Janey had had a hard day. Darlene and Willie had been such pests that finally Pat had driven off in his car and killed time, sitting by the roadside reading magazines, feeling bored and worried.

Janey never liked shopping for socks and underclothes and dull things like that which she and Jimmie and May needed. She found the stores crowded. Furthermore, nobody seemed to want to wait on her, and stout, impatient housewives pushed ahead of her at counters. Also when she caught sight of her own reflection in store windows she disliked herself extremely. It was too cool a day for a rather mussed and outgrown flowered blue cotton dress and she wondered why she had put it on. She couldn't see one thing about her face that seemed attractive and she wondered, unhappily, if Pat didn't honestly think she was hideous and was just being nice to her, as he tried to be nice to his cousins, because he believed in peaceful co-existence. Probably when he went off to school he would forget all about her, and scarcely even speak to her during Christmas vacation. She had known this sort of thing to happen to girls, to some of her friends, actually, and when it did you wanted to hide in a closet and lock the door and simply never, never come out.

In one of the stores she saw lovely plaid wool skirts and matching cashmere sweater sets; a brown and beige skirt that was enchanting, and a red and brown and yellow plaid like autumn leaves. She wanted one of these so much that she felt she could scarcely bear not buying it. Almost never in her life had she wanted anything so much, not, she thought, since she was a small girl and had been obsessed and frantic with the desire for a little white icebox full of tiny artificial food. But that had been too expensive, as these skirts and sweaters were.

As she forced herself to leave that department to find the one where there was a sale on overshoes, she found that she was whistling softly, under her breath, *The Wearing of the Green*. Then she saw the store clock. It was nearly two and she had had no lunch. She finished her shopping in half an hour, realized she might have to wait twenty minutes for a bus and decided to telephone Pat and see if he wouldn't meet her downtown so that they could drive right out to hunt up those two girls.

It was pleasant to hear relief in his voice when she got him on the telephone. He would drive down at once, he said.

"I'll be on the corner of Church and Chapel Streets," she said. "Would you go to my house and tell Mrs. Kenney what we're doing, Pat, and please have her give you a sweater for me."

She hung up, dropped a lot of packages and had difficulty picking them up from the floor of the booth. Outside it, women glared at her wanting her to hurry. As she went out of the store, she wished she had time to pick up a sandwich somewhere, but everything would be so crowded she doubted if she would even be waited on and she mustn't keep Pat waiting. She seemed to be in a very depressed mood today and she even thought that those buttons probably didn't exist. To her dismay, after Pat picked her up and they had driven out of the city, he seemed as sunk in spirits as she had been. He said, "You know, I've been thinking you and I are like those deluded people who go chasing will-o'-the-wisps over swamps, and following echoes in woods, or the poor guys at the time of the explorers who were always trying to find the Northwest Passage. Hunting for things that weren't there. I wonder if we're wasting our time, Janey?"

This pulled her up out of her own depths. She sat quietly, thinking for a moment or two, while he drove on, accelerated, honked his horn once and passed a slow-going little car scarcely bigger than a toy. She said, "No, I don't think we're chasing things that weren't there. Mrs. Sally Green wouldn't go running after imaginary lights and echoes, and she definitely gave us the clue about the buttons and the ginger jar."

"So she did." He sounded a little cheered. "And we'll surely get on the track of that frightened guy when we show Jeannie Lee Ames and Kitten Grymes his white hat."

"Have you brought it?" Janey demanded, afraid that he hadn't.

"I have. It's in the glove compartment. Get it out."

She did so and held the dirty white object, turning it in her hands, studying it. It was the kind which had a brim turned up around the crown. "I can't make out any more names than I could yesterday," she said. "They're awfully smeared and blurred by the rain."

"Two names may be enough," he replied. "How shall we go about it? We don't want to have people think right off that we're crazy the way the Lexes and Aleshines did."

They both laughed. He slowed the car down a bit as they came up behind a truck.

"We'll just take the cap and ring the doorbell and ask for Jeannie Lee, or Miss Kitten Grymes—"

He snorted, amused.

"And when we see them we'll say that we found this cap, and want to return it to the boy who lost it and would they tell us his name and where to find him," Janey went on.

"Sounds a bit thin to me," he commented.

"I can't think of any better way, can you?" she said.

"No, I can't. We'll try the Ameses on Davenport Street in Branford first."

She felt uncomfortable about this and hoped it would not be as difficult as it had been questioning Lexes and Aleshines. "Oh dear, I do hope she won't be a horrid person," she said.

They soon stopped at 119 Davenport Street. The house was an old white frame one, not large, not small, well-kept with a flower border of marigolds and zinnias along both sides of the front walk. Both Pat and Janey got out, went up to the door, and rang the bell which was not a bell but chimes. Steps sounded quickly inside and the door was jerked open by a girl about Janey's age or a little older, blond, pretty and sure of herself. She wore red and black toreador trousers and a black sweater. For a moment she looked at Pat and Janey in astonishment.

"Hi!" she said. "Who are you?"

Pat seemed struck dumb. Janey said, "This is Pat McGill and I'm Jane Murray, from New Haven."

"Hi!" the girl said again and Janey wondered, wildly, if that were the extent of her vocabulary. But it was not. She said, a little irritated, "Well, what's cooking with you? Do you want to come in? Have I ever met you?"

"I don't believe so," Janey answered and held out the hat.

The girl drew back a little and asked, "What's that for?"

"Are you Jeannie Lee Ames?" Pat asked her.

"Yes, I am. What's that with the hat?"

"We found it," Janey said, "and your name was on it so—"

"Look, do you think I'd wear a dirty white saucer like that on my head? It's not my hat. I advise you to throw it in the garbage can. I wouldn't be seen dead wearing a thing like that!"

"We never thought it was your hat." Janey felt that this Jeannie Lee should be calmed down. "We know it belonged to a boy but since your name is on it we thought you might know who he is and where he lives so we can return it to him. That's all."

The girl took the hat and made a face. She turned it around in her hands. Her expression changed and Janey thought: She does know whose it is. She does know.

The girl looked up suspiciously and said, "You're going to a lot of trouble about this object, it seems to me. What's behind it?"

Janey hoped that Pat wouldn't go into the subject of the buttons, but she was afraid that if she poked him in the side to warn him he would ask what she was doing that for. But he said, vaguely, "Well, sometimes an autograph hat like this means a lot to a guy. Someone picked it up at my grandmother's place and Janey and I thought perhaps we could find the owner."

Jeannie Lee pushed it into his hands and said, "I don't know anything about it or—"

"But then how did your name come to be on it?" Pat asked quietly.

"I don't know. I haven't the least idea. I suppose everybody in school knows my name and somebody wrote it on for a joke. That's all I know."

"There's another girl's name on it, as far as we can make out," Janey said. "Kitten Grymes. Do you know where she lives?"

"Apple Tree Lane. It's an old gray house. Perhaps she'll tell you more than I can." Obviously Jeannie Lee was not too fond of Kitten Grymes. Obviously, too, she was tired of talking to Janey and Pat.

They thanked her politely and went on down the steps and back to the car. Dance music came from an open window at 119 Davenport Street as they drove away.

"She knew whose it was," Pat said and turned down a road leading to the water.

"I'm sure she knew," Janey agreed. "And she acted as if she were hiding something, as if she were afraid."

In five minutes they were parked in front of an old gray house on Apple Tree Lane. They went up on the porch and rang the bell and nobody came and nobody came and they waited and waited. Presently a thin old woman came around the corner of the house. "There's nobody home," she told them. "Kitten and the rest've gone down to the shore swimming." She disappeared around the corner of the house again.

"Well, shall we go home and call it a failure for today, or shall we hang around a while longer?" Pat asked.

Suddenly Janey realized that here it was toward the end of the afternoon and she had had nothing to eat since breakfast and was really quite dreadfully hungry. She told Pat and he said, "Poor Janey, I never thought to ask. It's a brute I am, and you're all the time feeding me. There's a little store just beyond here where they sell ice cream and stuff. Come on."

Presently they were standing at a counter in a country grocery store that smelled of cheese and crackers and apples and cardboard boxes. A very kind man in a white apron served them two large scoopfuls of peach ice cream, and Pat ordered doughnuts and cheese as well. With each mouthful Janey began to feel better. She had almost finished the ice cream when two or three girls came in, having left bicycles outside.

One of the girls said, "Hi, Kitten, didn't your grandmother say to bring her back some eggs?"

Pat and Janey turned and stared. The one called Kitten was small with a funny round face, blue eyes, and curly hair the color of a yellow cat's fur.

Pat wasted no time. He said to her, "Hi, do you mind telling me if you are Kitten Grymes?"

"Well, they call me that," she answered and giggled.

"Look," and he took the white cap from his pocket. "Your name is on this. Could you tell me the name of the guy this belongs to? We found it and I know that these autograph hats mean a lot to people and I'd like to return it."

Kitten looked at it, looked at Pat and then at Janey. She didn't seem to find them unpleasant characters.

"Oh, that's Allen Skidmore's," she said. "Skiddy's! Yes, he did like it a lot and he was all upset about losing it."

"Could you tell us where he lives?" Janey asked, politely.

"In one of those new houses on Marcey Street," she answered. "I don't know the number."

One of the other girls said, "There are two pink flamingos in the front yard."

"Thanks awfully," Janey said.

"Yes, we're very much obliged," Pat added. He was taking money from his pocket, paying the man behind the counter. He handed Janey the cap and they hurried out of the store and back to the car.

"The trail's getting hotter," he said, as they piled in and he started the engine. "Now I only hope that Mr. Allen Skidmore of Marcey Street and the two pink flamingos will be at home."

10

The flamingos were home, standing on the lawn of a brand new small, ranch-type house. Again Pat pushed a button, again chimes rang, again he and Janey waited. Finally there were footsteps, finally the door opened and an extremely small boy stood there. He must have been about seven or eight. Janey could sense Pat's disappointment.

"Look, brother," he said, "does someone live here named Allen Skidmore?"

The child said, "Sure, Skiddy, he's my brother. Why?"

"Is this his hat?" Janey asked.

"Sure, it's his dumb old hat. Why?"

"Could we see him for a few minutes?" Pat asked.

"You can see him, I guess, if you drive down to New York and take a taxi or a subway over to Brooklyn and walk to my grandmother's apartment on Henry Street. Skiddy's gone down there for the week end; it's his birthday and he's going up the Empire State building, and to see Radio City and everything. He always gets everything, Skiddy does, and I'm what they call the rejected child in this family, I'm the one that has the sibling rivalry they talk about on television."

Pat and Janey looked at each other. They had never met a character like this.

"Look," Pat said. "Would you know whether or not your brother Allen happened to find a lot of old buttons somewhere a few nights ago?"

Janey held her breath.

The child wrinkled his nose and sniffed. "Buttons?" he repeated. "I don't know about buttons. He found a piece of old broken china and took it up to school as the trophy for his initiation, and he said he found some other old junky stuff, in an old white sock, he said."

"Oh, could we see it?" Janey asked, desperately. "Look, could we see it? And perhaps buy it from you. We'd pay a lot for it."

The child said, "Well, I guess you can see it if you hunt around the cow and the calf for it, that's where he chucked it away, he said, he wasn't going to be bothered with keeping a lot of dumb old junky stuff, so he chucked it away."

Janey fairly moaned with misery and she heard Pat groan. He said, "Look, boy, where could we locate this cow and calf you speak of? Is there a farm near here? Is there a farm your brother would be apt to go to?"

"Sure, my uncle's got a farm out on Indian Trail Road."

"Does he have cows and calves?" Janey asked.

"Sure, he has cows and calves. Hundreds of them."

"What is his name?" Pat asked. "What is his house like?"

"Oh, it's a big sort of junky house with a lot of trees around it and red barns and there's a brook beside it. His name's Smith. I've got to go now, I've got to go and see

Reggy. He's got color TV, and we only have a plain one and that's not working. The tube's blown or something, good-by now. I'll be seeing you."

"Never again, I hope," Pat said, as the child ran past them and down to the sidewalk. "I never want to see that character again."

"What next?" Janey asked. "Shall we go home or what Pat?"

"We'll go out to the uncle's farm on Indian Trail Road. That's on the other side of Branford. So the 'old junky stuff' was in a white sock. That's what I saw him pick up from the floor and put in his pocket. I thought it was a handkerchief."

"Pat, do you think we can ever find it?" Janey asked. She felt tired and again discouraged, but Pat at least was not whistling *The Wearing of the Green*.

"We've come pretty close to it," he said.

"Yes, whatever the junky stuff was. Pat, you don't think it could be more little old Easter eggs, do you?"

"Gosh, what a horrible thought, Janey! No, I don't think so. Remember what Mrs. Sally Green said. I think they were Washington's buttons and, as I said, the trail is getting hot."

The trail might be getting hot but the day was getting colder with a wind rising and the skies a darker gray. They had to ask their way to Indian Trail Road and twice lost themselves and had to turn back. Behind the shore towns now they had come to open country, farm houses, stone walls and rolling fields. It was late in the afternoon and Janey thought they should be going home, or at least that she should telephone Mrs. Kenney and tell her where they were, but she didn't want to ask Pat to stop at some house so that she could go in and ask if she might use their telephone.

Once at a turn in the road they suddenly came upon a herd of cows being driven toward them by a small boy with a stick. Pat braked quickly and they sat there, surrounded by the big, horned creatures with large eyes and brown and white hides. The cows mooed and pushed and jostled each other and some bumped against the car. There were several half-grown calves among the crowd.

Pat raised a hand in greeting to the boy and called out, "There's a tick on that poor beast's neck. Better take it off, hadn't you?"

"Thanks," the boy called.

"Is there a Mr. Smith's farm near here?" Pat asked.

The cows had passed with the boy following; he turned and walked a few steps backward, calling, "Sure is, follow this road for two miles and then turn down Indian Trail to the right."

They went on, leaving the sound and the pleasant smell of cows behind them.

Pat said, "That's one thing I miss in this country of yours. It's so mechanized. I miss the animals. In Ireland, of course, on the farms, they're as much a part of the life as your own family. And on the roads you're always coming on flocks of sheep baaing and pushing each other, or herds of cows, or a family of a mother goose with a lot of little geese following in a line along the road. Or maybe there's a man on a bicycle driving an old horse beside him, or a boy going somewhere with three little pigs."

"With a horrible big gray wolf following them," she

interrupted. "I'll huff and I'll puff and I'll *blow* your house in."

He laughed a little, but not very gaily. He said, "One of the few things I remember about my mother is sitting on her lap by a peat fire and having her tell me that story. I used to love it."

"Particularly when the wolf fell down the chimney, splashing into the great iron kettle," Janey said.

They laughed and turned at a crossroads where a wooden sign on a high post said, *Indian Trail Road.*

It was scarcely a road, more a trail really, Janey thought. It was very muddy and bumpy and she could imagine Indians with feathered headdresses trotting silently along in single file, perhaps to attack Mr. Smith's house and red barns by the brook.

Soon they saw the house set among trees, and they rattled over a small wooden bridge and went slowly on past the stone wall in front of the house.

"If the cows are already in the barn being milked, whatever will we do?" Janey asked.

"Go up to the barn or to the house and ask where they are kept in pasture," Pat answered.

Janey groaned and said she could scarcely bear asking any questions that would make people think they were crazy, and Pat said that was one of the occupational hazards of this search. They had to steel themselves to meet the worst and not mind what people thought.

"I know," Janey said. "My father is always saying, what does it matter what 'people think'? What does it matter 'what people say'?"

"He's dead right," Pat agreed, "but not entirely. It matters a lot if the situation is serious. It matters tremendously if people think you're a thief. You can't just brush that off as if it were a crumb on your sleeve."

"No, you can't," Janey said. "Oh, where do you think they keep all those hundreds and hundreds of cows?"

The road had gone up a small hill and here was another curve.

"There they are. There!" Pat exclaimed. There was a bank along the road, then a stone wall enclosing wide, rolling fields. At some distance black and white cows were grazing. Perhaps there were calves but the animals were too far away to tell. Pat stopped the car.

Janey sat, feeling discouraged beyond words, but she didn't want to cast Pat into one of the glooms. She said, trying to speak in a matter-of-fact way, "Well, come on, Pat. We'd better begin."

"Begin?" he answered. He turned the key in the ignition switch and the engine died. "Begin?" he said again. "This is worse than searching through my grandmother's attic. It's worse than hunting up all those people and ringing their doorbells."

"Not worse than that," she said. "My spine fairly curled up when we did that. It felt as if it, and all the bones hitched to it, were curling up, you know, the way dead ferns do." She opened the door beside her, got out and stood on the road.

"Dead ferns!" Pat said, and laughed. He put the jingling keys in the pocket of his blue jeans and joined Janey on the road. "Okay, come on," he told her. "We'll never find anything if we stand here lamenting. Come along." A very narrow path led up from the road.

There was a smell of sweet fern and bayberry. They

climbed up the bank and pushed between clumps of goldenrod and wild purple asters. Tall sumac bushes with their rust red decorations of small berry clusters were along the side of the wall.

The wall itself, composed of hundreds and thousands of big rocks, was gray and white and, here and there, gray-green with lichen.

"Think of the men and boys who cleared the fields and built these walls in the first place," Janey said, as she climbed up and stood on top of one solid rock and another that was inclined to tip and tilt under her weight.

Pat stood beside her. Wind blew her hair and she shivered a little. Pat had forgotten to bring along her sweater and now she was cold. It seemed to her that this afternoon's search had gone on for years and centuries.

"I suppose these fields were cleared and these walls made when Washington wore his brown broadcloth suit," Pat said. "Perhaps the man who owned this farm then took his sons down to New York to the inauguration. How would they have gone, Janey?"

"Perhaps by horseback, or coach and four, or more probably sailing down the Long Island Sound from New Haven."

"Well, come on," he said, and they both climbed down into the field.

Janey felt a few drops of rain in her face.

They walked through hummocky grass, through brambles, over outcroppings of rock, gray rock with streaks of white quartz. They kept their eyes down as they went along and watched their own feet in their sneakers. Once they stirred a rabbit and it went bounding away before them in high hops, its white tail showing.

"I hate to frighten things," Janey said softly.

"I too," Pat admitted. Then he stopped and looked at her and ran his hand through his hair. He said, "This field must be fifteen acres large. I suppose there are thirty cattle in it. Where did Skiddy 'chuck' the old junk he didn't want to be bothered with? I'd hoped that perhaps he just tossed them away near the wall where the path led. But it's nowhere around and we can never hope to explore the whole field with a fine-tooth comb. Never!"

They turned and walked back, still looking at the ground and now and then kicking at it, disconsolately.

"Hello there, you two!" A man's voice was suddenly shouting at them.

It was not, Janey thought with relief, a disagreeable voice. She felt that she could scarcely bear it if anyone were cross with them, tired as she now was.

A stocky, gray-haired man in farm clothes was striding through long grass toward them. As he came up Janey saw that he had a weather-beaten, pleasant sort of face. "Lost something?" he asked and joined them.

"Well, yes," Pat answered. "Actually we have. It's hard to explain."

"Why not try?" the man said. He had small gray eyes that looked amused, under busy eyebrows. "What could you two kids have lost in my cow pasture unless you dropped something from an airplane as it flew over. They do often, it's true."

"No, we didn't drop anything from an airplane at all," Janey replied.

"No, you see, we've been talking with a nephew of yours who lives on Marcey Street—"

"In that house with the pink flamingos," Janey added.

"Those blasted flamingos!" the man said. "I'd like to hand them over to the ash cart. What has my nephew Skiddy got to do with this?"

"Well, we didn't talk to Skiddy," Janey started to explain. "His little brother—"

"Mervin?" the man groaned. "He talks like a poor TV program. Did you get anything out of him?"

"Well, a little," Pat admitted. "We gathered that Skiddy had gone to visit his grandmother for the week end in Brooklyn, and that he 'chucked' away something that we want to get track of. He'd thrown it near one of your cows with its calf."

The man looked surprised and frowned a little. He said that was a funny thing for Skiddy to have done. Why come way out here to dispose of something. It didn't make sense. "Just what did he 'chuck away'?" Mr. Smith asked.

"It was some things in a white sock," Janey put in. "It might be little old Easter eggs, but we don't really think so." Then she realized that that sounded absolutely crazy, absolutely.

The man stared at her and repeated, "Easter eggs?" in a dazed manner.

"No, no," Pat said, desperately. "I'm sure they weren't Easter eggs. We think they may have been buttons."

"Buttons?" the man looked more dazed than ever. "Why ever should my nephew Skiddy throw a lot of buttons in my cow pasture?"

"Some of my grandmother's buttons, valuable buttons!" Pat sounded miserable now.

"Listen, kids, who is your grandmother?" Mr. Smith asked as if glad to grab hold of some rope of reasonable common sense.

"My grandmother is Mrs. Barrow, Senior, of Three Pines Island," Pat answered. Then he stopped.

Janey knew he didn't want to go on and tell this nice man that his nephew Skiddy had stolen Mrs. Barrow's buttons. She felt that the more they said and the longer they talked the more involved they all got. They were like kittens with balls of wool, becoming more and more entangled.

"Well, frankly, I can't make head or tail out of it," Mr. Smith said, and now Janey realized that he was becoming a little irritated. "Sure this isn't some stunt, some joke you're playing?" he asked a little suspiciously.

"Oh *no*, sir," both Pat and Janey answered together, and Janey went on, "it's most deadly serious, truly. A person's reputation, his whole reputation for life, depends on it."

"Who are you? What's *your* name?" He asked her.

"Janey Murray. I live on Maple Street in New Haven and my father is on the Yale faculty."

"I see," he said. "Well, I've got to get the cows in for milking, and it's beginning to rain harder and I can't stop to sort all this out now. I'm sure there's something behind it. But if my nephew Skiddy threw a lot of valuable Easter eggs or buttons away in this field, I advise you to wait until he comes home from Brooklyn and ask him just where he did throw them. It's a good deal of ground to cover without any idea where you're to look."

They said they thought he was right, that they were much obliged to him, that perhaps he'd let them come out next week with Skiddy and see just where the things were.

"Surely, come out any time," the man said. "Nice to have met you. Your grandmother is a fine old lady, young man. We've been on some boards and committees together. That your car, my boy?"

Pat said that it was, and said thank you.

"Glad to have met you two," Mr. Smith said. "Drive carefully. Traffic's apt to be heavy at this time of the day."

The traffic was heavy but Pat did drive carefully. The two didn't talk much on the way back. Pat put the top up but it leaked and rain blew in at the sides and by the time they reached Maple Street it was dusk and late for dinner, and they were very cold and wet with rain.

"Thanks, Janey," Pat said, as they got out of the car. "I think now we'll have to wait for Skiddy to come home and tell us just where he threw that white sock with the buttons in it."

"Yes, just where the cow was standing with its calf."

"Just exactly what did that dreadful little boy say?" Janey asked. She and Pat were standing by his car and she was hugging herself with her arms trying to get warmer. She was drenching wet and her hair was sopping and lank about her face.

Pat said, "The kid said that his brother Skiddy had chucked the old junk away by the cow and the calf and if we hunted around there we might find it. Better go in, Janey, you're soaking wet."

"I am," she admitted. "Thanks for—well, thanks for an interesting afternoon, Pat."

"It was interesting, at least." Then he laughed.

Darlene's voice called to him from the door of the terrace, "You're too late for dinner. You're awfully, awfully late, 'Poor boy, poor boy, beggar boy, thief.'"

They're as mean to him as they can be, Janey thought with indignation as she went through the hedge. But as she went in her own front door there was her father, extremely glad to see her, saying that he'd been a little worried about her. And Mrs. Kenney came out of the kitchen and said she'd better go right upstairs and take a hot bath and put on a good warm dress and come down. She'd kept soup and a chop and a lovely baked potato and some beans hot for Janey, and there was gingerbread and whipped cream for dessert.

I wish I'd asked Pat here for supper, she thought. She knew he would feel badly about having to wait until next week to continue the investigations. But as for herself she was not too sorry. She didn't want to ask people any more ridiculous-sounding questions. I'm pretty well tired of the whole subject of buttons, she thought, as she ran hot water deep in the tub.

11

The next day was Saturday and Pat would have to be leaving for school on Wednesday. His grandmother was better. His uncle and aunt and his cousins, with the exception of Darlene, were off doing this and that. It was in the middle of the morning, his aunt would be home around noon and Janey was baby-sitting with Darlene. Darlene was painting, quite sloppily, sitting at one of the terrace tables; Janey was sewing name tapes on Pat's clothes for school, and he was lying stretched out in one of the long chairs with his hands behind his head. The poodle lay in its favorite place in the petunia border. Perhaps he liked the smell of the flowers, Janey thought, and cut off another name from the long tape of them.

"Patrick McGill," she started to sew it. There must be names on every sock, on every shirt and pair of shorts and sweater, sheet and pillow case and towel. Pat's Aunt Cindy had asked Janey if she could help in putting them on. She would gladly pay a cent per name, but Janey, feeling that she was blushing violently, thanked her and said she would be glad to do it and wouldn't think of accepting money for it. Pat was very appreciative.

He said now, "I suppose that boy Skiddy might come home tomorrow afternoon. I think I'll call him up around supper-time tomorrow and see if he can tell us anything about the two bovines."

"What's a bovine?" Darlene asked.

"An animal," Janey said.

"What kind of an animal?"

"Four-footed," Pat replied. "Do you think that's a good idea, Janey? I hate to waste time."

"Yes, I think it's a good idea and I don't see what else we can do."

"Why are you two talking secrets?" Darlene asked. "Who's Skiddy?"

"A character from outer space," Pat answered. "I want to ask him some questions about bovines. He's been off to Mars for the week end."

"No, to Grand-Mars," Janey said. She knew it was a pretty poor joke but Pat laughed.

Darlene said, whining, "You're teasing me. It's mean. You're both mean, and everybody knows you stole those buttons."

Pat looked at her angrily. He said, "Everybody's mistaken then. I thought that a person in this country was supposed to be innocent unless proven guilty."

"I don't know what you're talking about," Darlene whined again.

Inside the house the telephone rang and Pat hoisted himself up and went in, slamming the screen door behind him. Darlene jumped up, knocking over the glass of paint water and spilling it all over the table, and the glass rolled off and broke on the tile floor. She ran into the house after Pat, and Janey put down all her sewing things on the floor and quickly followed Darlene.

The telephone was in the "Reading and Television Area" in an L-part of the living room. Pat was sitting at his uncle's desk with the instrument at his ear. He was saying, "This is Pat McGill, right. Who's speaking? So what? Who are you? I don't like anonymous calls. What makes you think I'm hunting for something?" There were pauses between his sentences and he was listening, frowning. Darlene perched herself on a corner of her father's desk and kept demanding, "What is it? What is it?"

"Hush," Janey told her. "Be quiet." She felt rather frightened.

Pat said into the receiver, "Okay, you've got your point across. You've told me I'll never find what I'm hunting for, and warned me to lay off. Carry on further. What'll happen if I don't choose to lay off?"

A rough voice rumbled on faintly from the instrument. Pat looked more and more serious. He said, "You say the things have no value anyway. Then why are you in such a flap about them?" He listened. "Okay," he said, "okay, is this your idea of a joke or is it a threat? Hello, hello, hello." Then he looked at Janey and said, "He hung up."

As he stood up they heard the front door open and close.

Darlene cried out, "Marmee, Marmee, Pat and Janey have been perfectly horrid and talking secrets all the time and talking all about bovines and space men and Mars, and now somebody called up and I think he threatened to kill Pat—"

Mrs. Barrow came into the room looking very smart in a new wool dress and with her hair just set. Darlene jumped off the desk and clung to her.

"Please, honey, don't drag on me," her mother said. "What is all this, Pat?"

"It's Darlene's imagination that's slipped its brake again, Aunt Cindy."

"Oh well, what can you expect when a child has as much imagination as Darlene has? I think she'll be a writer some day. Janey, dear, how are you coming along with the name tapes?"

"There are still a good many, Mrs. Barrow, but I'll get through them."

Pat said, "Aunt Cindy, do you suppose my grandmother is well enough to see me if I go right down to the hospital now? I'd like to take her some flowers."

His aunt said, "Oh yes, I'm sure they'd let you see her for a few minutes, and you can pick a nice little bunch of petunias from the border for her if you want to. Wouldn't you like a peanut butter sandwich before you go?"

He thanked her and said he thought not. He'd get a milk shake or something in the drugstore downtown. Then Mrs. Barrow said she'd brought something home for Darlene and told her to come into her room and try it on. They went off down the corridor to Mrs. Barrow's room.

Janey asked, "Who was it on the telephone, Pat?"

"I don't know. Some guy who disguised his voice to make it sound very tough. I have an idea it was the one who came with Skiddy that night and kept telling him to bring along a trophy."

"Was it really a serious, I mean, a dangerous threat?" Janey felt more than ever frightened.

"Well, he was trying to scare me off from keeping on with the investigation. I'm not worried about the threat. What does bother me is what he said about the things not being valuable. What if there were just a lot of Easter eggs in that sock?"

"But why throw them away on Mr. Smith's farm?" Janey asked.

"Oh glory, I don't know." Pat rubbed his hand through his hair. "Come on, Janey, let's go down to the hospital and see my grandmother and ask her right out flatly if she can remember hiding those George Washington buttons in that ginger jar. She hasn't been up to seeing visitors until today but now, you see, it'll be all right."

"Shall I go out and pick some petunias for you?" Janey asked.

"Petunias!" he was scornful. "I'll buy her a dozen roses. I don't want my grandmother to think I'm a penny pincher."

"I see, well, come on then, Pat, but first I'll have to take your clothes and tapes and my sewing things back home and tell Mrs. Kenney I'm going to the hospital to see your grandmother."

He followed her out onto the terrace where they had to pick up the broken glass that Darlene had knocked over onto the floor. But in fifteen minutes they were off again in Pat's little car.

On the way down he stopped at the same florist's, and he and Janey went into the warm, sweet-smelling place with roses and chrysanthemums and gladioli in the showcase. Janey was shocked at the price of the roses and pulled Pat's sleeve and said that the button chrysanthemums were lovely and would last much longer and were far less expensive.

"I've only one grandmother," he answered, and gave the florist a five-dollar bill.

Janey went out, carrying the long green paper cornucopia of pink roses. When they were in the car and had started off again she thought she really knew Pat well enough by now to remonstrate with him gently for extravagance. She said, "You know Pat, money, well, I suppose you're not too familiar with our dollars and everything, but it does just melt away, and we do have to watch it, and you're going to be needing a lot of things for school, you know."

" 'Poor boy, poor boy, beggar boy, thief,' " he imitated Darlene. "I know very well you're thinking, poor boy, he shouldn't be buying expensive bunches of flowers when his coat is all frayed and ragged. Weren't you, Janey?"

"W—ell."

He said, "My grandmother's been good to me. All the years after my mother married, my grandmother wrote to her every month and she used to send me ten dollars every Christmas. She deserves roses and not just any old little bunch of petunias from the border."

"Of course she does," Janey admitted, "but—"

"You're still thinking about my ragged jackets, aren't you? I'll tell you something about all that. My father had a policy. Before he died he said to my guardian Dan Owens, 'Let the boy wear his old clothes, let him look like the ragged little old gray man under a blackthorn bush by the roadside. Then he'll soon find out who the men of good will are, the ones who stop and offer him kindness.' "

She didn't quite understand this and asked, "Could he have meant those little gray men under bushes in fairy stories? The two older brothers of a family always march by and pay no attention to him, but the youngest brother always stops and shares his crust of bread and piece of cheese, and then he turns out to be a prince in disguise—"

"Or else," Pat said, "he gives the youngest brother a golden goose or a purse that always has money in it, and then the generous youngest brother marries the princess."

"And all because he shared his crust with the little gray man," Janey finished, "who suddenly pulled off his long gray beard and flung off his long gray coat, and there he was a glittering son of a king!"

They both laughed but Janey felt that somewhere along the way she had lost the point of the story and she wasn't sure who was supposed to be the gray man under the blackthorn bush and who the kind youngest brother. She didn't want to ask Pat now because he was driving through heavy traffic, frowning a bit and going with great care. She was holding the cornucopia of roses on her lap and she put them up to her face and drew a deep breath, glad that Pat had bought them for his grandmother. But there was always something slightly mysterious about Pat. He was smiling now in an odd way and since they were going through an uncrowded street she asked him what he was thinking about.

"A nickname they gave my father in Ireland."

"What was it?"

"I'll tell you sometime. The hospital's down this street.

Oh blast, they've changed the traffic direction again. It's one way the wrong way! I'll have to drive around for miles and if I can't find a parking meter I swear I'll leave my car bung in the middle of the street and take the key."

"And lose your license," she said.

He glanced at her and laughed. They drove around blocks, finally found a parking meter, put in the dime and ran to the hospital.

When they got to Room 318, Mrs. Barrow, Senior, seemed very much pleased to see them and was truly delighted with the roses. She already had chrysanthemums and gladioli and a nice little bunch of petunias but no roses at all. Janey went down the hall to find a nurse's aid and a vase and some water and when she came back with the flowers arranged in a tall and rather unattractive jar, Pat was sitting in a straight chair by the bureau, having left the comfortable one for her.

Mrs. Barrow, Senior, was sitting up in bed, propped up by pillows. She wore a pink bed-jacket and her white hair was nicely waved. She looked an attractive but rather stern old lady. Janey had met her before and had always been a bit afraid of her.

"Sit down, child," Mrs. Barrow told her. "Put the roses on the bureau. Good of you to give them to me, Patrick. We're talking about where he is to go on his vacations," she explained.

Janey thought this wasn't exactly what he had come for but she did not say it.

"You see, I am flying out to California for the winter as soon as I'm on my feet again," Mrs. Barrow explained. "Patrick, my boy, perhaps you'd like to spend your holidays with some of your other uncles and get to know them and their families?"

"Ah, grandmother, I'll be all right," he told her. "I'm going to try again to persuade my guardian to open up my father's fishing shack in Florida for the Christmas holidays. I wish he would and maybe you'd come down there. It's on the Gulf, you know. I should think you'd like it better than California. Most people do."

She said, "That's kind of you, Patrick, but I've never been fond of fishing, and old ladies don't do too well in shacks."

"Well, it's—" Then he stopped and Janey wondered what he had been about to say.

Mrs. Barrow's voice sounded a little tired. She said, "Of course, your Uncle Will and Aunt Cindy and your cousins are delighted to have you with them, my boy."

"Yes, I know. Don't worry about it, Grandmother."

"Where are you sleeping, with Ronnie and Willie?"

"No, in the rumpus room downstairs. It's all right. It's quite comfortable and there's the small TV set."

"But there's no closet!" She sounded distressed. "Where do you keep your clothes, Patrick?"

"Ah, in my flight bags and suitcase. Why not? I've not many although Aunt Cindy bought the stores out for my school clothes. I surely hope my guardian sends her a check for them quickly."

"If he can't, my dear boy, I'll take care of it," his grandmother said. "I do hope you'll like your boarding school, Patrick. It's very important to make a good impression at the beginning, not to go with any sort of a cloud hanging over one's head."

There was a pause. He said gravely, "The last thing I

want is to go up there with any cloud hanging over me. And Grandmother, I've wanted very much to ask you—"

But he hadn't time to ask her anything at all for just then a doctor and a nurse came into the room and Pat and Janey had to leave. They went down the long corridors where there were nurses in white and aides in pink hurrying along in white rubber-soled shoes. Bells rang. A loud voice from an amplifier called for Dr. Newman. "Dr. Newman wanted on the sixth floor please, emergency."

"I certainly am glad I'm out of there on my own two feet," Pat said.

"I'm sure the nurses and doctors take wonderful care of one," Janey said.

"I'm sure they do, but still I'm glad to be out of doors going to my own car. Come on, Janey, aren't you starving? We'll stop at the drugstore and get something to eat."

They got in his car; he started and backed it out.

"When I was fixing the flowers, you asked your grandmother about the buttons?" she asked.

"I didn't seem to have a chance. You know, I've been thinking a lot about that anonymous telephone call," he told her.

"I don't like it."

He was driving down a very crowded street again. She thought he did extremely well in traffic.

"I think that character who called up is afraid we'll go to the police and he wanted to stop us."

"Would you go to the police, Pat?"

"We haven't enough on Skiddy," he answered. "Besides which I'd really hate to get him in bad trouble. He sounded so frightened, and I'm sure he didn't like what he was doing at all. I'm quite sure he 'chucked away' the 'junk' in the white sock because he didn't want to be found with stolen goods on him."

"I suppose so. But why be so worried if they were only dusty old Easter eggs?"

"That's one reason why I think he had something really valuable. Look, Janey, I'll treat you to lunch. I'm going to have a double hamburger and a chocolate and vanilla float. How about you?"

She said she would have the same and then she said they had better eat fast and hurry home so that she could spend the afternoon sewing on name tapes.

He answered that it was very decent of her, that he appreciated it. They had to drive around blocks and blocks to find a parking meter but at last they did and then went to the pleasant, crowded drugstore for lunch.

12

It was a lovely day, the next day, although a little cool and windy and the weather reports on the T.V. predicted a storm to break late that night. Mrs. Barrow, Senior, telephoned her son's house in the morning and asked her daughter-in-law if someone could go out to Three Pines Island soon and find certain dresses and coats which she would need for California. Mr. Barrow was on Long Island for a golfing week end, Ronnie and Kit had been invited for an all-day sailing party out of Branford and Willie and Darlene clamored to be taken on some sort of a treat. Although they were not too fond of Three Pines Island, still they seemed to think it would not be bad fun to go there today, if they could have a cooking picnic on the shore. Mrs. Barrow told Pat that he might ask Janey to come if he wanted to, which he did. She came over and asked if there was anything she could do to help, and Mrs. Barrow, in a long chair on the terrace, looked up from the Sunday paper.

"Do be an angel," she said, "and pack up the big picnic basket for us. You and Pat go into the kitchen and see what you can find. Get hamburgers or frankfurters from the deep freeze if you want. And don't forget matches and a frying pan."

Darlene and Willie came in with them and were pests, imitating Pat's accent, exaggerating it, and starting to chant "Poor boy, beggar boy" in unison until Pat threatened to sift flour over them and they ran off to tell their mother.

"Lovely companions they'll be on the island today," Pat said in disgust, and he added, "Bring your bathing suit, Janey. I'm taking along my swimming things. This may be our last time."

"For the summer you mean," she said, quickly. She was wrapping hamburgers up in aluminum foil.

"Well, yes, for the summer naturally. I didn't mean our last swim on this earth."

It was a small thing, but it worried her.

It was the middle of the afternoon when they reached Green Cove and quite a wind was blowing in from the Sound. The Greens' house was closed. Nobody came when Pat knocked loudly at the door.

Mrs. Barrow stood hunched up in her coat with her hands in her pocket. The blue kerchief over her head was not becoming. She was too sophisticated a person for kerchiefs.

"Dear me," she said, "I wonder where the Greens have gone to. I should have telephoned we were coming out. I hoped he would take us to the island in his motorboat. Pat, you'll have to row us. Is that your grandmother's Clam Shell at the dock?"

He said that it was, that it seemed rather low in the

water. It had something of a leak and he thought he would have to bail it. He took the picnic basket out of the car.

Janey thought that five people were a good many for the Clam Shell and it would be a hard pull for Pat against this wind and the waves that were piling up.

Pat strode on down to the dock and Janey ran after him. He carried the picnic basket and she had the frying pan. There was a good deal of water in the bottom of the Clam Shell and the bailing tin was floating around in it. Pat put the basket on the seat in the stern and asked Janey if she would bail with the frying pan. She didn't much like to use something you cook in for scooping up dirty water but she didn't want Pat to think her too fussy. They both took off their sneakers, rolled up their blue jeans, climbed down into the boat and began to bail.

Mrs. Barrow sat on the steps of the house and Darlene and Willie disappeared behind it.

"If we bail in unison," Pat said, "and get a rhythm and swing it'll go faster." He counted and they dipped in the can and the frying pan, scooped up the water and threw it overboard and dipped, scooped, threw again and again.

Janey said, "Do you think it's safe to take us all together with the leak in the bottom?"

"It's not too bad," he answered. "Hi, Aunt Cindy," he shouted. "Will you call the kids. It's okay now."

His aunt, however, didn't seem to think it was quite all right. She didn't like the water that was still in the bottom of the boat. There was not much but she didn't want to get her suede sport shoes wet, nor did Janey blame her. Mrs. Barrow sat in the stern holding the picnic basket, looking over it unhappily.

Pat had told Janey to sit on the small seat in the bow,

the two children next, and he rowed facing his aunt. Willie fussed and objected, saying that he didn't want to be squashed up with Darlene, he wanted to be the pilot and sit in the bow and tell Pat where to steer to reach the island.

"I know very well the course to the island," Pat said. "At present I'm the captain of this boat and you'll do what I order, young man. You and Darlene sit where I told you to and if you wriggle and fool around I'll cuff you when we get ashore. I mean it." He had cast off and was rowing out toward the entrance of the cove.

"You wouldn't dare," Willie said.

And Darlene cried, "Marmee, you wouldn't let Pat hit us, would you? Pat thinks he's so wonderful! He's horrible to us. He's always perfectly horrible to us!"

Her mother said, "Pat's the captain now, Darlene. Don't bother him." She closed her eyes and said, "Oh dear, I wish it were not so rough. I don't know why, after spending my childhood on the island I should still get seasick, but to tell the truth I never did like the water. Get us ashore as quickly as you can, Pat, won't you please?"

He was pulling, as it was, with all his strength. Janey felt that this wasn't going to be too pleasant an experience. She could tell, even from their backs and their hunched shoulders, that Willie and Darlene were sulking and cross. And poor Mrs. Barrow in the stern looked quite green with seasickness.

Further out when they had left the protected cove, there were white caps and several waves slapped angrily against the hull and broke spray into the boat and the children squealed and blamed Pat for soaking them.

"Let me row," Willie demanded. "I won't get Mother

all dripping. You don't know how to row, Pat McGill. Let me have the oars." He actually stood up.

"Sit down!" Janey shouted.

And Pat, glancing over his shoulder, roared, "Sit down, you landlubber of a puppy! Don't you know better than to stand up in a boat like this?"

It was an unpleasant and hard trip over and everyone was relieved when Pat pulled the Clam Shell into the little harbor of Three Pines Island and tied her up at the dock.

"Leave the things in the boat," Mrs. Barrow told Pat. "We'll cook an early supper in the outdoor fireplace. Willie, you and Darlene can play around outside. Pat, perhaps you and Janey can help me in the house."

But it was a pity, it was a great shame, Janey thought, and hoped that Mrs. Barrow wouldn't have many jobs for Pat because he was so anxious to put on his skin diver's suit and have his swim. He was wonderfully self-controlled and obliging, Janey thought, because he never even let his aunt see that he didn't want to be mewed up here in the big chilly house, bringing suitcases down from the attic, hunting with Janey for his grandmother's black winter coat in the cedar closet, hunting for Ronnie's checked sport jacket in various other closets, and, finally, helping Janey scour the bottom of kitchen pots and pans. Mrs. Sally Green had planned to come over and finish the cleaning next week.

Mrs. Barrow went into the kitchen to look around, investigated the cooking utensil cupboard and was horrified at the condition in which the Goodwards had left things. "Darlings," Pat's aunt said, "I simply can't go away and leave everything so perfectly filthy. I wonder that Mrs. Sally Green didn't check and attend to these, but of course she is getting very old and forgetful and can't see well. Look, my dears, there are rags and cleaning powders." She opened a door in a cupboard beneath the sink. "Do what you can to scour these pots. You'll have to use very little water because I'm afraid there isn't much in the tank and, of course, there's no electricity, and I know the telephone was disconnected three days ago. I'll have to go upstairs again and pack your grandmother's clothes."

She left them and Pat and Janey turned to work on the bottoms of the pots and pans and both of them now whistled together *The Wearing of the Green.* "It's one of the saddest songs in the world," Pat said.

"Are you feeling unusually sad?" Janey asked.

"Well, I did want a swim, you know."

Presently, as they were working away, they heard two voices out in the front of the house shouting, "Hi everybody! Hi everybody!"

"It's Ronnie and Kit," Pat said. "I wonder what they're doing here."

Janey said she was going to ask Mrs. Barrow if she'd like to have the pots and pans wrapped in newspapers and put in a carton for the winter so she went out and up the front stairs. She heard Kit telling her mother that it was cold and wet sailing and so she and Ronnie had asked their friends to drop them off here at Three Pines Island, and they'd go back to shore in the Clam Shell and Pat could take them all home in his car. Janey thought it would be quite a squeeze. She went along down the upper hall to Mrs. Barrow, Senior's, room with its wide view of the Sound. Kit and Ronnie were there talking to their mother who was taking things out of bureau drawers and packing them in suitcases. When Janey asked her about the pots and pans she said vaguely that she thought it would be a good idea to wrap them in newspapers but she didn't really care. So Janey went back to the kitchen and to Pat who had found a lot more roasting pans and muffin tins greatly in need of scouring.

Presently, Pat glanced out of the window above the sink and said a storm seemed to be blowing up, and it might be a wise move to go back early and not wait to cook supper here on the island.

He had just said this when they heard Mrs. Barrow crying out, "Oh, oh! Pat, Janey—go out and stop them, call to them, stop them!" Her voice was terrified.

Pat and Janey ran out of the kitchen and across the dining room and the living room. Mrs. Barrow was running down the stairs with Kit and Ronnie following. Ronnie was saying, "They're all *right*, Mother. The Clam Shell is the safest boat on the Sound. Don't get in a panic. Willie will be rowing her back in a minute."

"But it's so rough, it's so rough and the boat leaks!" Mrs. Barrow cried wildly.

Wind caught at Janey and seemed to be trying to push her back to the house as she ran down the path after Pat. When she came out from under the trees she saw a rowboat way out between here and Bayberry Bush Island. Two small figures were in it, one rowing, having a hard time for the boat seemed to be spinning around and around.

Pat was at the end of the dock, kicking off his sneakers.

"What are you going to do?" Janey asked, dreadfully anxious. The Clam Shell seemed alarmingly low in the water and, as she watched, Willie who was rowing lost one of his oars. "Oh heavens, heavens!" she said. "They can never get back now."

Pat said quietly, "Of course they will."

Mrs. Barrow and Kit and Ronnie came up, Mrs. Barrow weeping.

"Come back, come back, Willie, Darlene!" she screamed, cupping her hands around her mouth. "Come back," and then, to the others beside her, "Somebody *do* something!"

The sky now was all dark clouds and the wind was strong.

Pat had stripped to his blue under-shorts. He said firmly, "Don't frighten them, Aunt Cindy. I'll swim out to them and bring them in." He dived into the water, a long shallow dive and came up for breath some distance away.

Before she left home today Janey had put her bathing suit on under her clothes. In a minute now she stood on the dock's end ready to swim.

Kit said, "Don't go in, Janey. It's too rough. It's no kind of a day for a girl to try to get to the boat."

Ronnie said uneasily, "Gosh, there's no use my even trying it. I've never been able to swim fifty yards in a flat calm, but Pat's almost a professional at it."

Mrs. Barrow was crying and shivering, her knuckles pressed against her mouth.

Janey thought, "I'm almost as strong a swimmer as Pat is and he's going to need help." Then she held her breath and dived from the end of the dock.

At first the water was very cold and so rough that it was difficult to make any headway. Waves broke over her and she swallowed water. She couldn't see Pat's head, but she could see the Clam Shell, very low in the water, the two small dark figures now huddled together. "I mustn't let myself be frightened," she thought. "This is just swimming. I'm perfectly able to do this," but she wished she could make faster headway. If that bad place in the hull of the rowboat had given way more, if the water was pouring in, the Clam Shell might sink at any minute and would Pat be able to rescue two frightened, struggling children?

Now to add to the difficulty, it began to rain hard. She tried to swim mostly underwater, tried to swim fast, to push herself forward, to turn her head, blow out and breathe as she had been taught in the Y.W.C.A. pool. But water got up her nose and she choked and coughed, went down in black depths and came up again, shaking her head and coughing as if she were a beginner, awkward and terrified.

Ahead she saw the broken waves that indicated the Styx Channel. The name was frightening. She remembered what Pat had said that morning about the last swim and that was more frightening. Also she was tiring, and she couldn't see Bayberry Bush Island, the waves were so high now all about her. Nor could she see the Clam Shell. Had it sunk? And where were Pat and the children? She was almost frozen with fear.

Now she was so tired that she felt as if she were trying to swim in some heavy, sticky substance like molasses, like dark honey, submerged in it, caught in it forever, but then it broke over her face and was salt water. She kept telling herself that she was perfectly able to keep up, that it was childish to get in a panic. For a moment or two she did the old-fashioned breast stroke, craning her head up, like a turtle, as old ladies in the pool swam, and everybody secretly laughed at them. But this stroke had one advantage which was that you could see better. She found that she was approaching the rough water of the Styx Channel. In it, but still some distance away, tossing and pitching was the Clam Shell and, to her horror, the two children were standing up on one of the seats clinging to each other but teetering as if at any minute they would be thrown overboard.

Then she heard Pat's voice from ahead, calling, faintly, breathlessly, "Sit down, you little ninnies!"

And Willie's and Darlene's voices answered, screaming faintly, "Pat, Pat, Pat, the boat's sinking!"

Then she was caught in the strong swirl of the Styx Channel, pulled under, was able to come up again but not able to advance against the force of the water hurrying out into the Sound. She hadn't strength enough. It was as if she were trying to lift up a moving van. She simply hadn't strength enough. And the Clam Shell was being spun away, further out.

As she was thinking in despair that it was hopeless, that she was at the end of her strength and must give up, she heard Pat calling, "Janey, let the current take you along. Try to get to the edge of it and then swim down to the Clam Shell."

She stopped struggling, but kept her lungs full of air, relaxed and drifted, swept along but now not in conflict with the force of the water. Then she began to kick strongly and swim toward the right. Lifting her head, she saw that she had been carried past the Clam Shell, that the children were sitting down in their seat and that Pat was swimming up to the boat.

In three minutes she too had reached it, and here the water was somewhat calmer.

"Are you all right, Janey?" Pat asked. His voice sounded hoarse and exhausted as if he were scarcely all right himself.

"I am," she gasped, treading water. "What shall we do now?"

In the Clam Shell the two children were sitting on the rower's seat and the food basket was still in the stern. Willie had his face in his hands and was whimpering and sobbing, but Darlene cried again and again, "I want Marmee. Pat McGill, you've got to take me right back to Marmee. You've got to take me right straight back this minute. Do you hear, do you hear, do you hear?"

Still treading water, he said wearily, "Just pipe down, Darlene honey, will you please. Janey, we'll have to push them into Bayberry Island. I'll get on the other side of the stern."

Even with two swimming and pushing the Clam Shell, it was not easy. The boat was heavy and although they were no longer in the fury of the Styx Channel the tide was running out, and now and then waves broke over them. They had all been carried out so far that they still had a hundred yards to go before reaching the Island.

"Janey," Pat said, "if she opens up and sinks before we reach shore you take Willie and I'll take Darlene. She's more apt to give trouble. You've had life-saving lessons, I suppose."

"I have." She was kicking hard against the water but she was pulled sideways and her knee came up against the hull of the Clam Shell and was badly scraped by some barnacles.

Darlene had heard him. She cried out, "Pat McGill, you can't let this horrid old boat sink on us. You've got to take care of us. Let go of it. You and Janey are pulling it under."

"Oh, pipe down," he said again.

Janey thought he was almost done in.

"Put your feet down," he said. "Put your feet down, Janey."

She did so and felt blessed sand beneath her. Bayberry Bush Island shelved out gradually. Staggering, it seemed for miles, through the suck and drag of the submerged sand and the surf, they managed to pull the boat up onto the beach.

The children were safe now. Pat and Janey stood catching their breath. The shore and the gray sky seemed to Janey to be circling around her, opening and shutting, silently clapping themselves together. She felt so faint and sick that she had to sit down quickly to keep from falling. And she realized that Pat was also sitting down beside her with his head between his knees.

He said wearily, "I never could have done it without you, Janey."

"You could," she answered. "At one point I thought I had just given you a third person to rescue." She was shivering now with the cold.

"And at one point," he replied, "I thought you were going to have three people to save."

It was then that Darlene did something unexpected. She had climbed out of the Clam Shell and ran up and flung her arms around Pat's neck and plumped down into his lap. He hugged her. "You saved our lives!" she cried out. "Pat McGill, you saved our lives and I think you're perfectly wonderful and Willie and Ronnie and Kit and I've been mean to you. We've been horrid to you and I don't see why you didn't let Willie and me drown, and I'll never sing that mean skipping song again. Oh Janey, I'm so cold and I feel so sick and hungry. Do something— do something. And I don't know what's the matter with Willie, he just sits there in the boat and shivers and moans."

"Shock," Pat said, and stood up. "Janey, we've got to manage to get these kids warm and we've got to show Aunt Cindy that they're alive and all right."

But when they went over to the Clam Shell and Pat lifted Willie out they saw that although he was certainly alive he was far from all right. He was a very bad color and as cold as ice.

13

As soon as Pat put the small boy on his feet the child crumpled up and lay on the wet sand, still shivering. All four of them, in fact, were shivering, but none of the others were as badly off as Willie.

Pat looked down at him with a worried expression. He said, "We'll have to warm him up. I imagine there's a more sheltered place on the other side of the island. Janey," he asked anxiously, "did you put matches in the basket?"

She said that she had, and some old newspapers and four sticks of kindling as well. Her father had taught them to do this for a cooking picnic because the wood one found was often apt to be damp.

Pat picked up Willie and held him in his arms as one does a hurt dog. He asked Janey if she could manage to bring the basket and the frying pan and she said that she surely could and Darlene declared that she'd help her.

"I could carry the food basket all by myself," Darlene said. "It's as light as a box of corn flakes. It's as light as one corn flake!" She seemed eager to be helpful and this was a comfort. Janey felt that she and Pat were surely in need of help.

There was a lot of water in the row boat. The frying pan was nowhere to be seen. Janey climbed in over the side, and was up to her shins in water. The place which she had scraped on the barnacles stung in the salt, and she noticed that blood was trickling down her leg. She handed the food basket out to Darlene who found it heavier than any box of corn flakes, but she staggered up the beach with it. Janey feeling around up to her shoulder in water found the frying pan and climbed out. With her wet hair blown about her face, and her wet, tight bathing suit she felt colder than she had ever been in her life.

She took the picnic backet from Darlene and gave her the frying pan. They followed Pat up the rise of ground that had bayberry bushes along the top. Janey now remembered how worried Mrs. Barrow must be. Although now the light was so gray and the clouds so lowering that it was impossible to see details on Three Pines Island, Janey felt sure that the Barrows were watching with binoculars. She stood on the crest of the little hill with Darlene beside her. They both waved and Janey tried to indicate with her motions that all was well. She and Darlene clasped their hands over their heads as fighters do when they have won in the prize-fighting ring. She very much hoped that poor, frantic Mrs. Barrow would see and understand.

In a minute now they were down with Pat and Willie in a small place sheltered by the rise of ground and the bushes. Here sand had been deeply scooped out by winds. Willie was sitting by a bush, still looking ill and pale but not quite so badly as he had at first.

"Find as much driftwood as we can." Pat said, "Bring it here and I'll build a fire and then a shelter. See if the matches are all right, Janey."

She answered, "I put them in a little glass jar and screwed the lid on tight. They should be dry."

"I'm surely glad of that," he answered. "Will, boy, you stay here and buck up now. We'll have you warmed by a fire in no time. It's always pretty tough at first when mariners are cast away on a desert island and then it gets to be fun."

"We're Robinson Crusoes!" Darlene said. "Four Robinson Crusoes. Janey, we ought to have a parrot and a goat. Come on, let's get some wood." Her pretty little blue cotton dress was drenched and limp and her hair had come out of its pony-tail and was straggling around her face, but yet she seemed to Janey a far nicer child than ever before.

There was a great deal of driftwood on the shore, some, near the water, was too wet to burn, but plenty of it half-buried in the dryer sand and more under the bayberry bushes seemed to be possible fuel. There were parts of heavy planks with large spikes in them, four rungs and two sides of a ladder, an old broken kitchen chair, some long beams, a crate mostly in pieces and a lot of chunks of varied shapes and sizes. The best discovery of all was when Darlene came upon a battered old door.

She called out, "Somebody come help me carry this."

Pat and Janey ran to her and Pat said, "That's as valuable as treasure for us, Darlene. Good for you for finding it."

"Can you possibly break it up and burn it?" Janey asked.

"It would be hard," Pat answered. He knelt beside it and pushed and scooped off sand that had covered one end. "But it's perfect to help build the shelter," he said. It had once been painted white but the paint was blistered and peeling and one side was charred.

"It was in a wreck," Darlene exclaimed. "It was a door in a burned boat and probably all the passengers and the crew had to jump overboard into the flames and sharks ate them." She seemed delighted at the thought.

"I doubt it," Pat replied. "Come on now, let's carry this back. I want to get the fire going and poor Will warmed up."

When they got back to him he was sitting hunched up with his teeth chattering.

Janey said, "Oh Pat, I don't know what's the matter with me. I never remembered the hot chocolate in the thermos bottle. I should have given it to him right away."

"Do it now," he told her, "and give Darlene some too. We don't want her succumbing on us after being so wonderful."

Darlene beamed and offered to help him start the fire. Janey unpacked the basket, laying things out on a level bit of ground. The matches were in the small glass jar. Darlene took them, some crumpled newspapers and the kindling sticks to Pat who was kneeling and scooping out a hole in the sand. There were three quart-sized thermos bottles, one for chocolate, one for coffee and one full of cold water.

Janey said, "Pat, I really think coffee would be more of a stimulant for Willie. Do you think it would be all right for him?"

"I do," he answered. He was building up a structure of

sticks over the paper and kindlings and Darlene was crouched beside him.

Four different colored plastic cups one inside the other formed the cap of the coffee thermos bottle. Janey unscrewed these, took out the cork and poured coffee out into the red one for Willie. She was relieved when he roused himself, took the cup and drank.

"It's good," he said and managed to smile at her weakly. "Can I have some more?"

She replenished his cup, then filled the blue one for Darlene and the green for Patrick.

"Ah, my own color," he said, taking it, smiling at Janey. "Swallow some down yourself, girl," he told her. "If it were polite to say you're pale as a slice of cod, I would."

"You're absolutely green, Pat McGill," she answered, but not in an unkind tone.

"I assume the green like a chameleon," he answered. "I'm such a patriot of my own country. Look, Darlene, sit this way a little and keep the wind off the fire. It's a lazy flame in there. We'll have to encourage it."

The coffee nearly burned their throats as it went down but it was delicious, very sweet and quite strong. It made Janey feel like a new person. She collected the cups, put them back in the basket and then helped Pat blow on the flame beneath the sticks and twigs. Willie revived a little and joined the other three. They all lay flat on their stomachs, blowing gently. Suddenly the small flame leaped into a strong blaze, burning the paper, the twigs and then the kindling. Pat ordered Darlene to bring him the next-sized pieces of wood and she handed him slats from the crate and then heavier chunks.

"Break up the chair and the ladder," he told them,

and when Darlene began to try to break up the chair, Willie jumped up and took it from her and beat its legs on the ground.

"Is he strong enough?" Janey asked, anxiously. "Shouldn't he just sit and rest by the fire?" That's what she herself wanted to do; just sit as close to it as she could get and put her head down on her knees and let the warmth flow through her while she rested a little. She felt that she would give anything in the world if she could suddenly find herself sitting here wearing, instead of the skimpy bathing suit, her usual clothes: good high socks, thick rubber-soled shoes, a tweed wool skirt and cashmere sweater set. In spite of the coffee and the fire she was feeling extremely tired now and limp.

Pat was saying to her kindly, "Come on, Janey, let's build the shelter. You'll feel better too when you stir around, and as soon as the fire dies down some, we'll cook the supper."

"I don't feel like eating a mouthful, Pat," she told him as she stood up.

"You will, though, in a few minutes. For myself I could eat the cow and the calf too."

And how odd it was, Janey thought, that for hours and hours they hadn't thought of the George Washington buttons at all.

Pat put more wood on the fire and then with Janey's help set about building the shelter. The straight side of the small hill formed one wall and the door set in the sand along on its side at right angles to the hill made another strong wall. Opposite this, perhaps six feet away, Pat and Janey pushed up a sort of rampart of sand for the third wall. Then Pat pulled up and broke off the tallest of some dead bayberry bushes and with these and three long poles of driftwood he roofed over the shelter. By now it was dusk. The fire was burning well and Pat told Janey he thought she might begin her cooking. Then he walked down and joined the children and Janey saw their three figures gathering up armfuls of dry marsh reeds and some seaweed strewn along the sand at the high water mark.

Now Janey wiped sand out of the frying pan with a paper napkin, unwrapped the ground meat from its aluminum foil, salted the pound and a half of hamburg well, put it in the frying pan and set that carefully on two thick slabs of wood that had fire under and between them. In a minute or two a delicious smell of cooking came coiling up from the pan and mingled with an equally delicious smell of wood smoke and burning resin. Next, she turned her attention to a real treat: corn on the cob, eight ears of lovely young corn. She didn't husk it but she did take off most of the brown, soft corn silk and then she laid the ears in the dying embers.

Pat and the children came back with their arms full of reeds and grass and seaweed. Willie seemed almost to have recovered, and he and Darlene shouted out, "When can we eat? When can we eat, Janey? It smells marvelous! It smells wonderful!"

"Nothing's ready yet," she told them. She knelt on the sand, turning the meat over with two long forks and the heat was a delight.

The children dropped their bundles of grass and Pat took handfuls of it and placed these in orderly rows on the roof. He said, "If I had time and rope or some wire, I'd make a regular thatching job of this. One of the very ancient men in our village at home taught me the art of it. Not many know it now. I could make my living thatching roofs if I wanted to."

It was hard for him to cover this roof, small as the area was. He had to push up between the bayberry branches, sticking his head and shoulders out. Darlene and Willie handed the reeds and grass to him, and he worked quickly and deftly.

And it wasn't long now before Janey said that supper was ready. She got paper plates and the picnic forks and knives from the basket. Pat put a roll on each long fork and toasted them while Janey served the hamburgers and managed to pull the corn away from the heat. There was butter in a glass jar. And now everybody thought it would be pleasant to have the hot cocoa. Now it was dark and the tips of flames seemed to break off into sparks and go sailing away up toward the sky.

The four sat beneath the roof of the shelter, protected from the wind, warmed by the fire, and ate the hamburgers on toasted rolls and stripped the corn, spread butter and salt on it and gnawed along the wonderful lines of tender kernels—sweet and buttery and salty, all blended with a faint taste of wood smoke and perhaps a little flavor of resin. They made places in the sand for the plastic cups to stand in. The cocoa was piping hot, as indeed were the corn and the hamburgers.

The children sat between Pat and Janey, so close that it was difficult to move an arm freely, but it was warmer and cozier to be so huddled up together.

"I never knew that it could be such fun to be cast away on a desert island!" Darlene said. "Janey, could I have another ear of corn? It's marvelous, it's wonderful. I bet this is the way they cook it in the best New York hotels. I bet it is, isn't it?"

Janey didn't laugh at her, but she said she thought they probably had different ways of cooking corn.

"Well, I think you're the best cook in the world, Janey," Willie said, and added as gruffly as a small boy's voice can be, "and I think Pat's the best swimmer and rescuer and shelter-maker in Connecticut and—"

"In Connecticut?" Darlene cried indignantly. "I think he's the best in the United States, Willie Barrow."

"Well, I do too," Willie replied angrily. "You keep still, Darlene, I'm trying to say something. You never will let me say *any*thing!" His voice rose and suddenly he took his half-eaten ear of corn, which was one of the longer ones, and bashed his sister Darlene over the head with it.

She wept wildly and tried to throttle her brother, crying out, "I've butter in my hair—all horrible salt and butter in my hair!" Cocoa cups were spilled. Pat and Janey pulled the two children away from each other.

"Look, kids, look," Pat said. "Peaceful co-existence now. Peaceful co-existence."

"How can I be peacefully co-existent with Darlene when she's so mean to me!" Will cried. "She's mean to everybody. And, Pat, I'm *sorry* I've been horrid to you. I think you're the best swimmer and the best rescuer and—"

"Well, thanks a lot," Pat cut in and stopped him. "I certainly appreciate it. Look now, Darlene honey, stop crying. Who's going to toast marshmallows on these long forks?"

Janey went into the shelter on all fours, searched and

found the box. In a few minutes the smell of toasting marshmallows mingled with the smell of salt water, of seaweed and smoke.

Everyone began to feel sleepy, and the children leaned heavily and warmly against Pat and Janey.

She said quietly, "I wonder when we'll be rescued, Pat?"

He answered, "I've been thinking of that. Nobody is home at the Barrows' house on Maple Street. And the telephone has been cut off from Three Pines Island, and the Greens may be away for the night and not know that we came out to it today."

"Well, we're wonderfully comfortable now," Janey said. "The children's clothes have just about dried on them."

"Won't your father be worried, Janey?" Pat asked.

"Yes, he will be and I suppose that by now he'll be trying to telephone around and get a line on us. But I don't think he would remember about the Greens at Green Cove, and of course he can't get through to the island. But I suppose that he may call the Coast Guard. Poor father!"

"You and the kids had better go a little further back into the shelter and go to sleep. I'll keep the fire up all night."

"But you'll have to have some sleep. Pat, you must be absolutely done in with all you've been through," she suggested.

"I'm not though," he answered. "I was a bit before dinner. But I'm so thankful that the kids are safe."

"And reformed characters," she said softly, and smoothed Darlene's head in her lap.

"They always were good kids," Pat said. "Well, I'd better be moving around and gathering some more wood." But he didn't move immediately. He sat staring into the flames and in a minute he began to whistle *The Wearing of the Green*.

"Pat, what's the matter?" Janey asked quietly.

"It's the buttons, the blasted buttons. And is Skiddy back yet and will he be willing to take us out to his uncle's farm and show us where he chucked them away? And are they buttons, or are they Easter eggs?"

He stood up then and in moving roused Darlene who opened her eyes and yawned.

She said, "Pat, do you think that tomorrow morning you could bail out the Clam Shell and help us row to the Cow and the Calf? I know Willie feels awfully because we didn't get there this afternoon, but it is a long row and it was so rough."

Pat and Janey exclaimed together, "The cow and the calf!"

And Janey said, "How in the world could you *row* to the cow and the calf?"

Willie was awake too. He yawned and said, "The Cow and the Calf are rocks, of course, outside of Branford Harbor. They're rocks, they're just rocks, one big one and one little one."

"The big one's the Cow," Darlene informed them, "and the little one's the Calf, and Willie and I were trying to row there and we were going to find the buttons that that boy threw away."

"How do you two know anything about this?" Pat demanded, amazed.

"Oh, we just listened," Darlene said. "We always listen to what everybody is talking about."

"But you shouldn't," Janey told her. "It's not at all a nice thing to do Darlene. It's not right!"

Willie said, "I guess it's right, isn't it, for spies to listen every time they get a chance to? Darlene and I are Private Spies, Incorporated, I don't know exactly what that means, but we're spies not private eyes."

"Spies not eyes, spies not eyes," Darlene chanted.

"My word!" Pat said. "The Cow and the Calf! What do you know, Janey? What do you know about that?"

"I'm sleepy, I'm dreadfully sleepy, Janey," Darlene said. "Please come inside the shack with me and keep me warm. Pat, is your fishing shack in Florida like this one?"

Janey was aware of a laugh behind his voice as he answered, "Something, and it's a bit larger, but not nearly as elaborate."

"Not as elaborate as this—oh poor Pat!" Darlene sounded shocked.

"What do you mean, it's not as elaborate?" Willie asked.

"Ah well, it hasn't any wonderful doors in it from wrecked vessels, and it hasn't any lovely thatched roof and none of its walls are of sand or big bonfires like ours here."

Willie was sitting up, clasping his hands around his knees, looking into the fire. "I think this is the nicest house in the United States," he said firmly. "I don't think there is any other house as nice on this planet or on Mars either. I'll bet there isn't. Pat, I'm awfully sleepy."

"Listen!" Pat said, suddenly.

They were all quiet and in the quietness they heard the sound of a boat's motor approaching.

"We're being rescued! We're being rescued!" Willie cried.

Pat picked up a short bayberry branch, put the end with twigs on it into the fire and when it caught and flamed, he ran with it up the small hill behind the shelter. The others followed him.

He seemed very tall to Janey as he stood there, waving the blazing torch.

People shouted from a long shape of a Coast Guard boat offshore. Then a searchlight came on, its beam moving, and a rowboat was in the light. Pat and Janey and the two children felt blinded as the beam shone full on them.

They ran down to the shore where they had landed, where a large rowboat was being pulled up the slope by two Coast Guard men.

Flashlights moved from one person to another, and Janey saw, briefly, Mrs. Barrow weeping, and her own father looking strained and anxious. They got out onto the sand and there followed a tumult of exclamations, greetings, questions and explanations.

The young children hung onto their mother, and she kissed Pat and said, "I can never thank you enough, never. Janey, my dear, my dear!" She turned and kissed her and Janey felt poor Mrs. Barrow's cheek wet with tears. Janey's father's voice was husky as he put his arm around her shoulders, and said, "Well, child, thank these officers for finding you."

Everybody thanked them. Mrs. Barrow wanted to hear

all about what had happened. There was a great feeling of excitement there on the dark shore of the small island.

Darlene said shrilly, "Pat was perfectly wonderful. Marmee, listen to me, listen to me!" She hopped up and down jerking at her mother's arm. "Pat is the most wonderful person in Connecticut."

"No, in the U.S.A.!" Willie shouted.

"Come on, son, let's get you all back to your own island and you can tell us all about it," one of the Coast Guard men suggested. He started to swing Willie up onto his shoulders, but the small boy began to scream and kick.

"I don't want to leave our lovely little shack. Marmee, don't make them take us away from our lovely little elaborate shack. I won't go. I won't go!"

Janey explained, "Oh, Mrs. Barrow, he's tired out and half-asleep and dreadfully over-excited."

Everybody was trying to calm and soothe him. The Coast Guard man had stood him down and he was still weeping wildly.

It was Pat who managed to quiet him. He put a hand on his shoulder and said, "Come on now, fella, be a good guy. Shipwrecked mariners never howl when they're being rescued. They go home and are treated like heroes and are given banquets, and after a time they go back and revisit their island. Janey and I'll bring you and Darlene out here some day and we'll have another cooking picnic." It was he who lifted up Willie and carried him down to the boat.

There was no excitement about going back. Janey sat beside her father. He had taken off his jacket and made her put it on. They were all transferred safely from the rowboat to the large boat. But when they came to the

• 158 •

Styx Channel, one of the men said, "Bad bit of water here."

"I didn't think I could ever swim across it," Janey said. She felt her father give a little shudder beside her and he put his arm around her more tightly.

One of the Coast Guard men said, "Wouldn't care to try to swim it myself." He added, "Shall I put you all ashore on your island, Mrs. Barrow? Will you be all right there?"

There was some discussion about that. There was no light or water or food in the big house so it was decided that perhaps it would be wiser to wrap the children up in blankets and take them right back home to New Haven. They would stop at Three Pines Island, pick up Kit and Ronnie and the various bags and things and then go on and be landed at Green Cove.

"I'm afraid there isn't room in my car for eight of us, plus all the bags," Pat said.

There was more discussion. Mrs. Barrow said she would order a big car from the taxi place to take them in. She didn't care what time of night it was. Mr. Murray said that he and Janey would go back to the city with Pat in his car and he would drive because the boy was tired out.

Pat declared politely that he wasn't at all, he was ready to drive from here to Florida, but he sounded desperately weary and sleepy.

Then they came into the Three Pines Island dock and the searchlight beam picked up Ronnie and Kit coming down the path carrying bags and clothes.

"They're all right," Mrs. Barrow called out. "Everybody's all right, thanks to Pat and Janey."

Pat got out to help with the bags and Janey heard Ronnie say to him, "I'm sorry Pat—for everything. I should have gone after the kids."

"You'd have been crazy if you had," Pat answered. "You're a skier, not a swimmer. I just happen to be sort of a—a porpoise by nature."

"You're just wonderful by nature," Kit said and patted his shoulder.

For one instant Janey had a twinge of jealousy. She thought: Oh dear, he's the nicest friend I have ever had. Kit's so much prettier than I am, and she knows how to get along with boys and have them like her, and perhaps she'll grab Pat's friendship.

But he was saying, "It's Janey who deserves all the credit. Don't forget, Janey, you're driving home with me and we have that date for tomorrow."

That chased away her unhappy feelings. She was blurred with drowsiness on the way to Green Cove and she slept from there to Maple Street in the back seat while Pat slept in the front beside her father who drove Pat's car.

14

Nobody wanted Pat and Janey to go out to Green Cove again the next day. Everybody treated them as if they were the most delicate of babies, or very old people. Willie and Darlene were kept in bed because they seemed to be coming down with slight colds, at least their mother thought they were and sent for the doctor. Mrs. Barrow wanted him to see Pat too and prescribe some good vitamins and listen to his chest to be sure he hadn't picked up something. But Pat was horrified at the suggestion.

He said, "Oh gosh, please no, Aunt Cindy. There isn't a thing the matter with me. I feel fine. I do, truly. It wasn't anything I did last night. Why I could swim three times that far and never feel it. And I've made small shacks ever since I was a kid. Honestly!"

He escaped then to Janey's house where Janey and her father were having breakfast in the kitchen breakfast nook. Mrs. Kenney, who was a nice small woman but not much of a talker, nodded and smiled at Pat and said, "Breakfast? Eggs? Bacon?"

He was going to say, no thanks, but Mr. Murray said, "Sit down boy, and eat."

"Please do," Janey invited him.

So he sat with them and he and Janey told Mr. Murray more about last night's adventures. He wasn't a man who ever said very much but he made them feel that he was proud of them both. Pat found that he was extremely hungry and was much stronger after the eggs and bacon, the tea and English muffins and marmalade. Mr. Murray said he had to rush off, got up from the table, took out his wallet and took bills from it.

He said, "Here, Janey, some Fun Money from my last sale of benches. Buy yourself some clothes with this—not just stockings and galoshes and dull things like that, but something you really want."

"Oh father!" she exclaimed. "Could I get a plaid skirt and a sweater set?"

"Anything you want. My grandfather used to say to my aunts, 'Go buy yourself a gold and silver doo-daddle.'" Everyone laughed. He kissed the top of her head and started for the door.

Pat said quickly, "Mr. Murray, may Janey come with me out to Green Cove this morning? I want to see if Mr. Green will take us out in his motorboat."

"It's a terribly important project, Father," Janey assured him.

"Well, if you feel up to it," he answered.

"Oh, we feel up to it!" They told him, in unison.

"Very well then. Have a good time." He went through the door into the pantry, and the black cat Ebon came in proudly and rubbed against Pat's legs.

It was early afternoon when Pat and Janey found themselves at the cove again and Mr. Ben Green was able to take them out in his motorboat. He and his wife and his mother-in-law, Mrs. Sally Green, had come home late that morning and been told by the next door neighbor about last night's excitement on Three Pines and Bayberry Bush Islands. While Pat went upstairs to change into his skin-diver's suit, Janey sat in the Greens' interesting, old-fashioned parlor and answered their many questions about what had happened the night before.

"So you think that boy Skiddy, whatever his name is, threw those buttons away near the Cow and the Calf rocks off Branford Harbor?" Ben Green asked when Pat came downstairs.

Janey always thought Pat looked like a man from outer space in his very tight garment of a material like black rubber and with the heavy weight-belt around his waist. His mask with its snorkel was pushed back on the top of his head and he carried his green fins in one hand and a flashlight in its underwater container in the other.

He stood in the doorway and said, "I think Skiddy threw something away there; something tied up in a big white handkerchief. He didn't want it to be found on him. I think he and his friend came out to Three Pines Island that night in an outboard motorboat from Branford Harbor, and on their way home he chucked the loot overboard, whatever it was."

Ben Green said thoughtfully, "It may be."

"I'm sure he had no intention of robbing anyone," Pat said. "I suppose whatever he threw away—well, I suppose, he just didn't want it."

"Perhaps he thought it wasn't worth anything," Janey suggested.

"I'll bet it was those buttons," Mrs. Sally Green said. "I'll bet you anything," and she nodded her head.

Her daughter-in-law was a stout, kindly woman who sat on the sofa and listened and agreed to whatever anybody else said.

"Well, come on, what are we waiting for?" Mr. Green got up briskly. "Come on, you two kids, if you feel up to any more stunts today. From all accounts you had quite an adventure last night."

They assured him that they felt fine, that really it hadn't amounted to anything. They followed him down to his dock and got in his boat.

It was a calm and sunny afternoon, a little cool, but not too cold. Ben Green took another course and did not pass very near Bayberry Bush Island. Last night might have been a terrible experience, Janey thought, but really it had been rather fun, in spots.

Presently, having rounded a long point and run along far out but parallel with the shore for a few miles, they saw the indentation of land that was Branford Harbor. Ben Green headed the boat more to the northwest and in a minute they sighted two dark objects above the surface of the water.

"The Cow and the Calf," Ben Green said.

Janey began to feel breathless with excitement. She said, "Oh Pat, why didn't we think to telephone Skiddy and ask him to come out here with us, or at least to tell us what the things were he threw away and just where he threw them?"

"I tried four times this morning to get his house on the

telephone," Pat replied, "and nobody answered. How about anchoring near the rocks?" He asked. He was putting the green fins on his feet.

"In the lee of the Cow," Ben Green answered. In a moment he cut the motor, then from under the stern seat brought out a small anchor and carefully let it down overboard.

The boat rocked gently and there were sparkles of sunlight sprinkled over the water.

"Oh I hope he finds them! How I hope he finds them!" Janey thought and twisted her hands tightly together in her lap.

"Okay," Pat said. "Thanks. I'll swim over to the Cow and then go under and scout around it. Don't worry if you don't see me as soon as you think you should. I may come up on the other side of the rock. Do you two mind trimming ship so I can let myself in. It's not too easy to dive with the mask and snorkel. Janey, will you hand me the flashlight when I'm in?"

She and Ben Green sat near the port side of the boat while Pat manoeuvered himself over the starboard gunwale, let himself down and reached up his hand for the underwater flashlight. Janey gave it to him and he swam over toward the Cow.

First he circled the larger rock, making an above-surface survey, trying to put himself in Skiddy's place on that night of the affair on Three Pines Island. They would have been coming down from it to Branford Harbor in their boat, approaching the rock from the southeast. It was a dark night and presumably they were in a small boat without a searchlight. They had an electric torch Pat knew. He came to the rock and hoisted himself up on a ledge of it, moving carefully so as not to tear or puncture a hole in his skin-diver's suit. He sat there, just above a fringe of seaweed, clasping his knees in his hands trying to figure out this problem. The sun was warm on his back. He thought: Now why did Skiddy chuck the stuff overboard here when he had had the whole Sound to throw it into before reaching here? Something must have frightened him. It may have been something the other boy said about stolen goods, or perhaps—ah, perhaps they saw a boat coming out of the harbor and thought they might be questioned. Perhaps it was the Coast Guard cutter. If it was they surely would be stopped. The guard would want to know what two boys of their age were doing out on the Sound at that time of night. Skiddy would have been frightened and, as they turned in toward the harbor, he'd throw whatever he had overboard. The course led in past the east end of the rock, past that part which looked vaguely like the Cow's head. Possibly Skiddy wanted to be able to find the stuff again, or to tell someone else where to find it. The best place to look would be below the head of the Cow.

Having arrived at this good conclusion, Pat waved at Ben Green and Janey, adjusted the mask over his face and went down into the water again. He had his electric torch tube ready so that he could have a beam of light for exploring when he submerged.

If he only had an aqua-lung, he thought! If he *only* had an aqua-lung and didn't have to come up all the time to breathe! And he should have added more lead plates to his weight-belt for he had to go deeper than he had expected. The underwater horizon faded into brown; the beam of light caught glistening particles. A fish flicked by. The rock rose black and unevenly beside him with ledges and crevices and floating seaweed around it. He thought he saw something white, off to his right, but he couldn't investigate now. He had to come up for air. He had stayed under almost too long and when he surfaced he was gasping.

After a minute or two he went down again with his torch lighted. His groping hands were white before him, and the white streak below was only a deposit of quartz or something, not the handkerchief with treasure tied in it. Disappointment gripped and weakened him.

He came up again, pushed back his mask, clung to the rock with his finger tips, breathed and rested. As if from far away, he heard Janey calling anxiously, "Pat, Pat, are you all right?" He turned, saw the boat bobbing gently up and down, and he waved and called that he was all right.

What a fine girl she was, he thought, and a grand companion if you wanted a good time, or if you were in trouble.

His mind shifted again to the problem at hand and he thought perhaps his reasoning was wrong. He would circle both the Cow and the Calf, underwater.

He did this, slowly, surfacing often, submerging, directing his light beam down into the black depths of water at the rock's base, playing it along at higher levels. He came back to the Cow's head, again clung to the rock with his head out, again thinking, deeply discouraged. His reasoning must be all off. Perhaps, after all, Skiddy had thrown his loot away on his uncle's farm on Indian Trail Road. Perhaps Pat would be able to reach him by telephone and ask him about the place tonight.

He decided to give it one more try before stopping and admitting he had failed here, so he fitted his mask back and went down again.

Now, as his beam of light felt its way downward and into a small crevice, he saw something white at the bottom of the cleft and quickly reached in his left hand. It may just be quartz, he told himself. It may just be that. I mustn't be disappointed. His fingers touched something that felt like cloth and then he had to come up again. It was maddening! He breathed, went down, thrust his arm into the hole to his arm pit. Undeniably, he felt cloth, grabbed it, drew the thing out and surfaced with it in his hand. Seldom in his life had he felt such joy.

It was not a handkerchief, but a sock that had once been white, and its toe looked like that of a Christmas sock that has been "hung by the chimney with care" and half-emptied. I won't open it until I do it with Janey, he thought. And as he swam back toward the boat he was in dread that they would find only Easter eggs or some such silly things in it. But Easter eggs surely would have melted long ago, he reassured himself. It couldn't be Easter eggs!

He reached the boat and held onto the gunwale with his left hand which also held the flashlight tube. "Take it," he told Janey and reached the dripping sock out to her.

He had never seen a girl look as excited, as jubilant. She and Ben Green were exclaiming together, and Ben helped Pat into the boat.

"Open it," he said. "Go ahead, Janey, open it! But don't, for Pete's sake, lose anything."

There was a strong string tied tightly around the sock.

Ben Green had to cut it with his pocket knife. Things rattled as Janey poured round metal disks into her lap.

"Are they?" Pat demanded. "Are they, Janey?" He made his way carefully down toward the stern and looked over her shoulder.

There were certainly buttons in her lap, but were they from George Washington's brown broadcloth suit? Janey was examining one.

She said, "I think they are not the awfully valuable ones, Pat. I think they're his inaugural buttons." Her voice was sorrowful, and she went on, "You see, they have G.W. in an oval in the center, but they don't have the seal of the United States."

"No," he agreed, "and they say that the lost ones on his suit did have the eagle bearing a scroll in his beak, and on the scroll *E Pluribus Unum*."

Ben Green, who was looking at them, said, "But I'll bet these are plenty valuable at that."

"And twelve of them," Janey said, "even if they were worth only ten or twelve dollars apiece, comes to a good deal. Pat, are you terribly, dreadfully disappointed?"

He was a little disappointed, of course, but he said, "No, I'm not, Janey. I'd rather have had them be the others from Washington's own suit, but what I really care about is that now the family will be convinced I'm not a thief and a robber and a vandal, and I'll not have to go up to school 'with a cloud over me,' as Grandmother said."

"A cloud over you, I should think not," Ben Green said. "The whole Barrow family ought to go down on bended knee to you and Janey for what you did for those two wild kids last night. Well, I'm glad you found these things, Pat. Stick them back in the sock, Janey.

I've got to be turning around and making for home. It's getting rough again and we don't want to be soaked on the way back."

They were not soaked but it was a bouncy return trip to Green Cove and no one tried to talk much above the noise of the motor. Moreover, both Janey and Pat felt extremely tired. But he, sitting relaxed up in the bow, felt more content than he had in months. He didn't want Janey to be sorry for him about the buttons. There wasn't any need.

Safely at Ben Green's, Pat felt fine, dressed again in his own clothes and his raggedy old tweed jacket, with the buttons safe in their sock in his pocket. Going home to New Haven, he felt so sleepy he had to keep his attention firmly fixed on his driving, and Janey actually dozed with her head leaning against the back of the seat, all the way from Green Cove into town.

He hadn't meant to be so late. He was afraid that the family would be eating dinner by the time he got there. Janey woke up yawning, as he turned into the Barrow driveway.

"Thanks a lot, Pat," she said. "I'm awfully glad you found them. Will you be over tomorrow? I still have a million of your name tapes to sew on." She felt a little as if she wanted to be whistling *The Wearing of the Green*.

"Come on in with me and see the family's reaction," he answered. "Janey, I hate to have you slaving over those name tapes. I'll hire somebody to do them."

"Oh ridiculous!" she told him. "I can do them in one morning. You mustn't fling your money around like that." Again she felt there was something mysterious about Pat and his finances.

He laughed a little, and together they went into the house. He took the sock out of his pocket and held it in his hand.

The Barrow family were at the dining-room table. They looked up and hailed the two with exclamations of relief. They said they'd been worried about where they were and why they were so late, and where had they been, and weren't they hungry.

Pat said, "We've been out to Green Cove and the Cow and the Calf, and we found what we've been looking for."

He untied the string from around the sock and poured the buttons out on the table beside his uncle's place.

"What are these, my boy?" Mr. Barrow said. "Good gracious, they're not very clean objects, are they, for the dining-room table?"

"A bit primitive!" Kit said with disapproval and then, leaning over and examining them, she gave a scream. "Buttons!" she cried, "G.W.—George Washington buttons. Grandmother's George Washington buttons!"

"But not from his brown broadcloth suit," Pat explained, "not the very valuable ones."

"But still these may be worth a good deal," Janey put in and felt that she could explain the situation perhaps better than Pat could. She said, "Skiddy, one of the boys who broke into the house on Three Pines Island that night, stole them out of Mrs. Barrow's ginger jar like Mrs. Lecks and Mrs. Aleshine, and then because he was afraid of being caught with the loot he threw them away by the Cow and the Calf, and Pat swam around them today and dived under and found them."

The Barrow family looked completely bewildered. "I don't quite get the score," Mr. Barrow said, "but I'm sure it must make sense. Pat, my boy, I'm glad you found them. And by the way, I think I have something of yours. It may be in my pocket." He felt in his pocket and brought out a small object. "Mrs. Goodward picked it up somewhere in the Pines Island House, I believe." He sounded embarrassed as he put something into Pat's hand.

Darlene was clamoring to know what it was.

Pat said, "Ah, it's just an old button of one of my ancestors. I always carried it as a lucky piece. I rather think that Mrs. Goodward found it in my pocket and drew the wrong conclusions." His voice was a little stern.

Mr. Barrow said, uncomfortably. "I'm more sorry than I can say, Pat. We owe you a world of apologies, and when I think of what you and Janey did last night to save these two worthless items of mine," he nodded at Willie and Darlene, as his voice choked. "When I think of that—well. . . ."

"It was nothing that we did!" Pat broke in. "Uncle Will, it was just a swim Janey and I took. You know there's nothing we like better than swimming."

"And I've got to rush home!" Janey said quickly, knowing that Pat wanted to be extricated from this scene. "It's dreadfully late. Pat, don't you want to walk me to the hedge—there might be wild bulls, or wild lions or something."

"So there might. A dangerous strip of grass that is. I'll be back in a minute, Aunt Cindy, if you'll excuse me."

Then he and Janey were safely out of the dining room and away from the embarrassing gratitude and thanks.

When they reached the hole in the hedge, Pat said, "Look, Janey, there are sure to be dances and things like that at school. Perhaps you'd come to some of them with me?"

She answered, "I'd love to, Pat. I'd simply love to!"

"And I'm going to try to persuade my guardian to open the Florida shack for the Christmas holidays and perhaps you could come down then—I mean, perhaps my guardian would get up a party."

She didn't think that was very possible, but she said that she would love it. And, anyway, the thought of a dance at St. Ronan's school swept her spirits up to the skies.

"It's been exciting, hasn't it?" he said.

"It's been frightfully exciting, a bit frightening in spots, but really wonderful."

"Buttons!" he said, and laughed. "Good night, Janey, thanks a lot. I'll be seeing you."

15

The name tapes were the next problem, but Pat's aunt, and Kit and even Darlene, struggling with her needle, helped Janey sew them on. It was all accomplished. Pat's new clothes and old ones were packed, and Mrs. Barrow drove him off to the school in Jefferson, Connecticut, on Wednesday. They started earlier than they had expected, before Janey was up to say good-by. She felt lonely and would have felt worse had there been time, but at noon her young brother and sister, Jimmie and May, came home from camp, brown and gay and with a hundred things to be done for them.

The Barrows' schools, and the Murrays' also, began the next day.

Janey felt that she was swamped in mountains of homework and had very little time to think of anything except Algebra and Social Studies and English Composition. She wore her navy blue school tunic over a tailored white cotton blouse, white socks and good tan leather crepe-soled shoes. Everybody in school was required to dress alike, and the Sisters—it was a Catholic school—preferred to have the pupils' hair cut very short or worn in pony-tails. So Janey put the elastic again around her hair and the style did not become her at all.

One afternoon in mid-October, coming home from school laden down with books, she encountered Kit Barrow. The two saw very little of each other, but they had had more friendly feelings for each other since the Bay-berry Bush Island rescue. However, Kit looked at Janey now with a critical, older-girl expression on her face and said, "Honestly, Janey, must you wear your hair pulled back like that? Can't you tell the Sisters, or whoever, that the style is just too primitive. Truly, you all look ante-diluvian, like cave women or something."

Janey felt a little hurt, but she laughed and said, "Can you imagine my going up to Sister Mary Genevieve and saying that to her?"

"I don't know why not," Kit answered, and then asked, casually, "Have you heard from Pat at all?"

"Well, yes, I have," Janey admitted. She didn't want to tell Kit that he wrote every week, awfully nice letters full of funny descriptions of boys and happenings, but dread-fully badly spelled and written. She wouldn't want Kit to see them.

Kit said, "Did you know that his guardian is going to open Pat's father's little place down in Florida for the holi-days? Pat asked all of us to go down there, but Father'd already taken a house on Biscayne Bay for us all for the Christmas vacation. And anyway, I'm afraid it would be pretty primitive living in Pat's fishing shack."

"I think it will be fun," Janey answered, feeling somewhat annoyed. She shifted her books under the other arm. "I think a fishing shack sounds wonderful. I can't wait to get there."

"Are *you* going?" Kit asked, astonished.

"Yes, Mr. and Mrs. Owens—he's Pat's guardian—wrote Father and said they were going to be there with Pat and they invited me, and I'm going."

"Well, for heaven's sake!" Kit was more than ever astonished. "Well, I hope you have a wonderful time, Janey. Perhaps we'll see each other down there."

"Perhaps we will," Janey answered politely.

"Take plenty of rough clothes," Kit told her. "Darlene says that Pat told her all about it and that his shack is roofed over with tar paper and has only three sides to it."

Janey thought this extraordinary and hardly possible. Then she remembered the conversation that night in the shelter on Bayberry Bush Island. She said, "Pat did say something about his fishing shack but I don't think he meant it to be taken literally."

"Well, perhaps not," Kit admitted, "and you can't always depend upon children's ideas. They've had a fearful crush on Pat ever since the Bayberry Bush Island affair, and they're awfully sorry for him because his father peddled bottled lemonade."

"Did he really?" Janey asked.

"Darlene asked him and he said so. He said he bottled it and, you might say, peddled it."

"It seems very odd," Janey said. "Thanks a lot for your suggestions about my hair and the clothes for Florida, Kit. You know a lot more about those things than I do."

"Oh well, I hope to be a model some day," Kit answered, "although I'll probably marry first." She nodded in a kindly manner and went on down Maple Street, while Janey went into her own yard and into the house. She felt very much puzzled about Pat.

She stood before her mirror, took her hair out of the ponytail and brushed it until it framed her face softly. In spite of what Kit says, she thought, I shall take a really nice dress or two to Florida.

The weeks passed and Pat did not come back to his relatives for Thanksgiving. St. Ronan's didn't allow the pupils to go home just for that one day but celebrated it in the school. When Christmas vacation arrived, Pat went straight to New York to his guardians and flew with them down to Florida. The Owens wrote and telephoned to the Barrows and Mr. Murray, and it was arranged that when the Barrows went south to their house on Biscayne Bay, Janey should fly down with them. Then within a day or two they would drive her over to the Gulf Coast, to Marathon, where Mr. Owens would have a motorboat meet them to bring them all out to Lemon Key. The Barrows would spend the day there and Janey stay on with the Owens and Pat.

Janey felt a little badly about leaving her father and her small brother and sister for Christmas, but they had been invited to spend it with cousins up in New Hampshire, in a lovely big house in the skiing and coasting country, and Jimmie and May were to stay on there until Janey got home and school opened again. Her father would have some free time to write, and the children would be happy so Janey could go off without feeling conscience-stricken.

"My dear," her father said to her on the morning before she left, "don't worry now, have fun. Young McGill is a boy I like and respect, although not everybody would understand him—I don't mean his accent because he hasn't much of one. But don't take his relatives' estimation of him. Make your own judgments about people. A ragged jacket isn't much of an indication of character."

"I know it isn't, Father. And his family like him much more than they did at first, and Darlene and Willie simply adore him now."

"Well, have a good time," he said again. He took out his wallet and gave her some more Fun Money, and she thanked him. He looked at her, with a question in his kind and worried eyes. "I hope you won't have a difficult time with the Barrows, but you won't be spending much time with them. They're not exactly our kind, but you're good with people. One has to get alone with all sorts."

"I know, Father," she agreed, "and I like them usually very much. Here it is Wednesday, and we'll be in Florida tonight. And they'll be driving down to Marathon on Friday to spend the day on Lemon Key and then I'll be there with the Owens and Pat for Christmas!" She could scarcely believe it, it seemed so dreamlike and wonderful.

"Well, have a good time," he said again, and kissed her. "Write to us, Janey."

At that, Ronnie and Willie Barrow appeared at the front door to help her with her bags. In ten minutes they were off in a taxi for the New Haven Airport to take a plane to La Guardia in New York. From there they flew to Miami and took a car to Biscayne Bay.

It was a little before noon on Friday when the Barrows, with Janey and her bags, drove up to the long dock in

Marathon, got out and stood looking about for Pat. There were some very expensive boats in the slips alongside: a lovely cutter named the Sea-Wind with two elderly people sandpapering the varnish; a smaller sloop, several large motorboats, newly painted and shiny, and a huge, ninety-foot houseboat with a crew hosing down the decks and sides.

"Don't see the boy, where is he?" Mr. Barrow said. "Hope we can all pile into his outboard motor dinghy, whatever he has."

"There he is. There, at the end of the dock!" Janey exclaimed excitedly.

A tall, thin, redheaded boy was coming toward them. He wore tan Bermuda shorts and a white shirt, tucked in, not a pictorial shirt flopping about his hips.

"Hi!" he said as he approached them. "Hi Janey! Hi everybody!"

He had lumped Kit with everybody, Janey thought, and she was glad.

He came up and shook hands with her, kissed his aunt, shook hands with his uncle, with Kit, and Ronnie. Darlene and Willie shouted *Hi's* and hung on him, and he patted them on the head and said gosh, he was glad to see them, gosh, it was swell that they could come down.

He was tanned and not quite as thin as he had been and looked wonderful, Janey thought, and happy.

"Where's your dinghy, my boy?" his uncle asked. "Can you pack us all into it safely?"

"Without any trouble," he answered. "Ah, here's Mr. Owens. Aunt Cindy, may I introduce Mr. Owens?"

His guardian was a bald, stocky man, a city sort of person, polite, but perhaps not too easy, Janey thought, to get along with, although when he smiled she liked him better. He smiled in a very kind way when he shook hands with her. Pat managed all the introductions as easily as if he had been seventy instead of seventeen. The Barrows seemed impressed and, in a way, a little daunted and silent.

Pat carried Janey's bags and everybody talked about the flight down as they walked along the dock. There didn't seem to be any boat that might be Pat's. A very smart motorboat with shining bright-work and red leather cushions bobbed in a slip at the end of the dock.

"Here's the Sionna," Pat said to Janey, with pride. "Sionna means Shannon, you know. There's plenty of room in her. I'll get in first, Cousin Dan," he said to his guardian, "and you can help them in."

They climbed down a few rungs of a ladder, were helped by Mr. Owens and handed carefully to their seats by Pat. Then they were all in, with Pat sitting in the bow at the steering wheel. This was no reluctant outboard motor to be started with a pulled string. A man on the dock cast off their lines, Pat thanked him, turned a key in the instrument panel, and the engine started with a soft purring. Pat backed out of the slip and they were off, cutting through the torquoise water of the Gulf.

"My word, this is some craft, Pat." Ronnie said. He was sitting opposite Janey, near the bow.

"Oh it's, it's the estate's." Pat did not turn as he answered.

Mr. Owens sat beside him. "It's Patrick's boat," he corrected. "As Lemon Key is Patrick's island."

"My word!" Ronnie said, almost under his breath.

The Sionna seemed to leap through the water. Willie and Darlene squealed with pleasure. Mrs. Barrow took a kerchief from her purse and tied it over her hair and, as usual, it looked badly on her.

Janey's hair blew about her face, but she didn't mind. It was cool and she was glad she had on her new soft white sweater. It went well with her dress—lemon yellow silk with very narrow stripes of white and pale green. It was well tailored and had not been cheap. Mrs. Barrow had suggested that morning that perhaps Janey was a little over-dressed to arrive at a fishing shack; they were all going to wear old blue jeans or some sort of everyday slacks and those Florida shirts with all-over designs of palm trees and amusing figures. She said that Kit could lend Janey a salmon-colored one with leaping swordfish if she wanted. But Janey had said, politely, that she thought she would wear a dress.

"Just how far away is Lemon Key?" Mr. Barrow was asking. Janey thought he looked a little foolish in faded tan trousers and a purple shirt decorated with cowboys. He seemed chilly too, with his shirt billowing out in the wind.

"That's Lemon Key ahead," Mr. Owens answered.

"But the—the house on it?" Mrs. Barrow asked. "Oh, I suppose you have neighbors, Pat."

"Not near ones, actually."

They were approaching an island and on it, among palm trees, was a most charming villa of stucco, a soft green color with white trim and with ornamental iron-work at the doorway and wide window sills.

"My word!" Ronnie said. "Fishing shack, indeed!"

Pat was coming into his dock. He said, "My father and I always called it that. It's on our letterhead. Now, in a minute, please, all ashore. Willie, my boy, don't hop out until I tell you to."

Everyone waited for Pat to help them out onto the dock. Janey, near the bow, stood next to Mr. Owens and Mr. Barrow and heard them talking in low voices.

Mr. Barrow was saying, "Well, Owens, it looks as if the Barrow families have not quite understood my nephew's situation. I realize now that we've always jumped to conclusions that his father was a poor man. We have heard rumors now and then that perhaps he was in the upper-income brackets but I'm afraid that my brothers and I were prejudiced. We thought that the wealthy one was some other Irish McGill. Even my mother didn't know the facts. And then Pat's clothes—well, you know, they didn't quite give the impression of money."

Mr. Owens made a small sound of amusement. He said, "It was my friend's wish that the boy should not be judged by outward appearances but by himself. Also he wanted him to be brought up as simply as possible under the circumstances."

"Some circumstances," Mr. Barrow remarked.

"Yes, Pat's father was one of the wealthiest men in Ireland. They called him the Lemon Squash King, and he sold his bottled lemonade all over Ireland, England and Europe. We're trying to open a market here in this country."

"A country grocery!" Mr. Barrow said. "Peddling!" Then he laughed, and Mr. Owens laughed rather grimly.

Pat reached down, took hold of Janey's hand and hauled her up onto the dock.

She said, "It's wonderful, Pat. You know, I always rather thought it might be like this."

He laughed and said his father had never liked a braggart or a boaster. "Look," he said, "we've got to loosen everybody up in some way. What's the matter with my relatives?"

Pat and Janey were walking up the dock together. She said, "They're frightfully uncomfortable because they haven't worn the right clothes. You see, they expected something 'primitive.' Darlene told them you had a sort of shack with a tar-paper roof and only three sides. I don't suppose they quite believed that, but they prepared for a roughish sort of day, and now they're rather appalled."

He laughed but not unkindly and said that clothes didn't matter, and that he and Janey and the Owens must just pitch in and give the Barrows the best time possible. "Come on, Janey," he said, "we'll put on a loosening-up program. The first item will be that everybody'll swim in the pool. It's not really a formal pool, just an excavated rough sort of area my father had dug out on one end of the island and fenced off from the Gulf with wire mesh so it's safe from barracuda and so on. But I must say I usually swim in deeper water outside."

"We did all bring our bathing suits," she told him.

In fifteen minutes everyone, including the older Barrows and the Owens, were in the protected pool, in the lovely, soft water with palm trees and blossoming hibiscus around the edge. Both Pat and Janey were careful not to seem so much better at swimming and diving than were the others. Presently, they came out and dressed and had luncheon on the terrace and the sun was warm, but not too warm. Everyone was relaxed now and happy and the food was, as Kit said, dreamily, out of this world and ter-

rifically civilized. There was grapefruit and orange cock-
tail, shrimp or chicken patties, avocado salad, hot delicious rolls, very buttery, and lemon sherbet and sponge
cake. Surely it had all been done by an experienced cook,
and it was served by a nice Irish butler in a white jacket.
Everyone had his own small table, and Pat and the
Owens went about and sat with this guest and that. Mrs.
Owens, a slim, gray-haired, garden-club person, was, Janey
realized, a very good hostess and invariably said just the
right thing to make one feel comfortable.

Pat made a special point of talking to Kit and then
joining his aunt and the small children. In between
courses Darlene and Will sat in his lap and climbed all
over him. Ronnie sat in a long chair and contentedly
looked at magazines: *The London Illustrated News, Holi-
day* and *The Dublin Opinion.* Mr. Owens and Pat's uncle
sat near Janey, smoking.

Mr. Barrow said, in a low voice, "You know, Owens,
I don't know quite what to do about the boy's Christmas.
I was planning to give him an aqua-lung."

Mr. Owens said, "So was I. It isn't the sort of article
you want two of. What shall we do?" He looked at Janey
and asked, "You know him better than any of the rest of
us, Janey. What would he like?"

"I'd be buying it with money from the Washington Inaugural buttons," Mr. Barrow said. "Even though they
weren't from the brown broadcloth suit, still I got a
pretty good price for them. How about it, Janey?"

She said, "I think it would mean a lot to him, Mr. Barrow, if you gave it to him for Christmas," and Mr. Owens
agreed.

It wasn't long then before they had finished their des-

sert and the Barrows said they must be leaving. They had
had a wonderful day but it was a pretty long drive back.
Pat and Mr. Owens took them in the motorboat to the
Marathon dock, but Mrs. Owens kept Janey on Lemon
Key to unpack and have a rest.

She helped Janey take her clothes out of the bags and
hang them in the closet. "I'm glad you brought such a
lovely dance dress," she said. It was pale yellow satiny material with some small roses embroidered here and there
on it, very full skirted and really most becoming. "Pat's
going to take you to the Junior Christmas dance at the
Yacht Club. Now, my dear, see if you can get a little
sleep. He'll want to have another swim with you when he
gets back."

An hour later Pat, in his black skin-diver's suit, and
Janey, in her candy-striped bathing suit, sat on the end of
his dock and watched the sun setting in the Gulf of Mex-
ico.

"It's wonderful!" Janey said. "Pat. I could never have
believed it would be so wonderful."

"It's pretty good, isn't it?" he agreed. "You know, I often think of all that button business. It was terrific in
spots but also it was awfully funny."

"What perfect maniacs we must have seemed to all
those Lexes and Aleshines! Pat, it was really screamingly
funny about the ginger jar."

"Please, could you tell us, Mrs. Lex, what your
mother-in-law did with the rent money fifty years ago?"
he imitated Janey's questioning.

They both began to laugh.

"And how absolutely ridiculous it was to be hunting
for the buttons on the farm on Indian Trail Road!" she

said. "No wonder Mr. Smith thought we were lunatics."

"Buttons—or Easter eggs!"

"And the Cow and the Calf! Taking a boat to the Cow and the Calf!"

It seemed funnier and funnier. "Buttons!" he said, "and ginger jars and cows and calves and Easter eggs!"

"And your primitive fishing shack with a tar-paper roof and only three sides!"

Then they swung their legs over the water and laughed until they nearly fell off the dock.